WE NEED TO DO SOMETHING

MAX BOOTH III

PMMP

Perpetual Motion Machine Publishing
Cibolo, Texas

We Need to Do Something

ISBN: 978-1-943720-45-3

Second Edition © 2021

PERPETUAL MOTION MACHINE PUBLISHING

www.PerpetualPublishing.com

Cover Art by Matthew Revert

ALSO BY MAX BOOTH III

Toxicity
The Mind is a Razorblade
How to Successfully Kidnap Strangers
The Nightly Disease
Carnivorous Lunar Activities
Touch the Night

PRAISE FOR
WE NEED TO DO SOMETHING

"*We Need to Do Something* is a single-location funhouse of horrors, starting off intense as hell and steadily tightening its grip. Unpredictable, unhinged and laced with offbeat humor, it's a confident and singular descent into domestic nihilism that's as wildly fun as it is deeply disturbing."

—Matt Barone, Tribeca Film Festival

"Works like a Pandora's box of horror. *We Need to Do Something* fearlessly takes risks, unwilling to play it safe."

—Meagan Navarro, Bloody Disgusting

"Unhinged, chaotic, and abounding with occult chills. *We Need to Do Something* is a nasty, violent, uncompromising slice of less-is-more horror, the kind that begs questions while offering enough conventional genre thrills to satisfy naysayers."

—Chad Collins, Dread Central

"I was greatly moved and entertained by the deceptively titled *We Need to Do Something*, but it is cursed art. By that, I mean that it elicits a powerful reaction out of you. So powerful that you'll probably never want to experience it again. This family trapped in a small bathroom undergoes such a tragic and terrifying ordeal, it's hard not to feel voyeuristic and, to a certain degree, terrified that it might happen to you someday."

—Benoit Lelievre, Dead End Follies

"Max Booth III is carving a niche out for himself as the king of premises that should not, in any way whatsoever, work. Yet, somehow, he does it. Every frickin' time. This novella shouldn't work, but it will absolutely wreck you. Get it. Read it. Love it."

—Anton Cancre, Cemetery Dance

"Given the short length of the novella, it is pleasantly surprising how much Booth has managed to pack into it. Complex familial relationships, witchcraft, hallucinations, and weird horror. Booth is simply continuing to prove what so many of his peers have already stated: he is one of the best authors writing horror today. Exceptional, fearless and, much to our benefit, only getting better with every story."

—Thomas Joyce, This is Horror

For Dylan

INTRODUCTION FROM THE DIRECTOR

Dearest Readers,

On June 18, 2020, I received a script written by Max Booth III that would very soon change my life forever. That script was an adaptation of the novella you are about to read.

At that time, we were three months into the strangest period I think most of us have ever lived through, and like many of you, I hadn't really left the house in what seemed like an eternity. For three straight months I was pitching projects to television networks and financiers that I felt could be done using archival footage, or remote capture—mostly documentary projects. And everyone kept acting like business was happening and projects were still being produced, and for a couple months I believed them. Then by month three—June—I knew we were all in denial, taking Zoom meetings and pretending like we were making things simply so we didn't lose our fucking minds.

Once I resigned myself to this fact, I started writing a script that I knew my partner Bill Stertz and I could produce using the resources we owned— cameras, a garage converted into a sound stage, some lights and random props left over from other productions. I'd directed a few documentaries, but this was going to be my first narrative film as a director. Made during a pandemic because I'm a fucking idiot.

Two days into this writing process—June 18, 2020—a gentleman named Ryan Lewis sent me a script that I had no interest in reading. Not because I didn't think it would be cool, but because I was hell bent on making the thing I was writing, in my garage. The next morning Bill messaged me very early saying something along the lines of "DUDE, DID YOU READ THAT FUCKING SCRIPT?". And I said something back like "NO DUDE, I FUCKING DIDN'T". We only message in CAPS, saying dude and fuck a lot. Obviously.

So at 6am that morning, I read it. Reluctantly. Pretty quickly, I realized this was something I could do within the exact parameters I had been writing for. Then I started connecting with the characters. Then I laughed a bit. And then, for the first time in my life, after reading literally thousands of scripts—I jumped. Words on a page produced a jump scare. It's an event in the script the few people who have seen the movie now tend to call "that moment". And from there on it got even better. Max was exploring themes that obsess me through his incredibly singular voice and worldview. And I loved every second of it. Now I knew, *this* had to be my first narrative feature—Max's words were the exact thing I'd wanted to do my entire life. I tossed that other script I was writing in the trash where it remains to this day. The genre Max perfected, and that Matt Barone from Tribeca Film

Festival would later coin "domestic nihilism", turned out to be very much my bag.

Shortly after this initial reading, the stars aligned: Hantz Motion Pictures came on board to finance, our incredible cast came together, and we all became a weird little temporary family who quarantined together in Southfield, Michigan to spend a month losing our collective minds inside a bathroom. Oops. Is that a spoiler? You did know this book takes place almost entirely in a bathroom . . . right?

This claustrophobic film was shot in isolation, during the height of the 2020 pandemic, under conditions that were less than ideal but that I wouldn't change even if I could. The book Max published while sitting on his toilet (true story!), about people trapped together in a confined space, would be shot by people trapped together in a confined space. It couldn't have been more beautiful.

This experience led to a friendship with Max and a bunch of other amazing artists who all made this movie together, and less than a year after first reading the script, we premiered the film at Tribeca Film Festival 2021—the first in-person festival since the pandemic began—outdoors under the stars on a giant LED screen in Brooklyn with a warm wind blowing in from the west. Yes, it was that poetic.

As you are reading this, our film has probably already been released in theaters by IFC Midnight. That means there are hopefully some people who love it, and lots of people who have trashed it. I'm happy with both responses—as long as everyone who saw it felt something visceral. Max's book pulls zero punches, leans into divisiveness as a rule, and is one of the purest artistic expressions I've ever had the pleasure of reading. So does his script, and if the movie does anything right, hopefully it's true to the fearless and audacious nature of Max's words.

I hope all of you find this book to be as riveting, hilarious, tragic, surreal, and truthful as I do.

Sean King O'Grady
Director of *We Need to Do Something*
July 29, 2021

EMERGENCY ALERT

TORNADO WARNING IN THIS AREA TIL 11:30 P.M. CST. TAKE SHELTER NOW. CHECK LOCAL MEDIA.

OUR PHONES WON'T stop screaming, each slightly out of sync with the other, making the noises jarring and insane.

We form a line and pile into the bathroom—Mom first, hugging a rolled-up blanket to her chest; followed by Bobby with a stack of board games nearly matching his height; then me, still soaked from the storm outside, walking on autopilot while jabbing my thumbs against the weather alert on my phone; and behind me, whiskey fresh on his breath, my dad. The only thing he's brought with him being his thermos. Nobody has to guess what's inside it.

"Oh my god," I say, turning off a new alert. Another one immediately generates in its place. Anxiety's threat of total annihilation increases with every additional pop-up. "*Why won't it stop?*"

Dad flinches, clearly annoyed by the pitch of my voice. "Just give it a second, would you?"

Mom motions for us to clear space so she can spread the blanket out along the floor. Pink flowers and butterflies decorate the fabric. The design has always made me nauseated. Grandma—on my dad's side—had gifted it to the family several Christmases ago. She also had always nauseated me. Yes, the way she looked and smelled didn't help, but it didn't end there. Her mannerisms were truly atrocious. The way she laughed could boil water. Once I heard her refer to those tiny black heads people get on their faces and necks as "n-word babies"—only, she'd actually said the word. Of course, Dad had thought that was the funniest thing in the world. Thank god for cancer.

Mom snaps her fingers until I look away from my phone. "Where were you? You should have been home by six."

Bobby plops down on the blanket and inspects his stack of board games as if, somehow, he'd forgotten one of his favorites.

I set my phone on the sink and attempt to dry my hair off with a nearby hand towel. "I told you guys I was doing homework at Amy's tonight."

Mom points at my arm. "What happened there?"

"What?" I follow her gaze and realize I'd forgotten about the band-aid. Amy had slapped it on for me, just below my inner elbow. There had been a moment earlier tonight when I thought it would never stop bleeding.

"Did you hurt yourself?"

I swallow, thinking fast. "Amy's cat scratched me. It's no big deal."

She waits for more. I offer nothing. "Why weren't you answering my calls?"

"I didn't hear it ringing." And, for once, it's the truth.

"You need to answer your phone when I call. That's why we pay for it every month."

I ignore this rerun of a lecture I've heard a thousand times before by retrieving my phone from the counter and cancelling the weather alert again, only for another to regenerate. "I told you, I didn't hear it ring."

4

"Not good enough."

"That's why I pay for it," Dad whispers, standing next to the closed bathroom door.

Mom turns to him. "What?"

The anger arrives in his eyes before it finds his lungs. "THAT'S WHY *I* PAY FOR IT. THAT'S WHY *I* PAY FOR THE PHONE."

We flinch and stare at him, wide-eyed, waiting for the outburst to progress. Mom shakes her head, dismissing the tantrum. "You know what I meant."

"Wow, Dad," I say, "what's—"

"—Mel, goddammit," Dad says, holding up his thermos to cut me off, "when we call your phone, you answer it. No excuses. Next time, you lose it."

"Okay," I say, then add under my breath, "god . . ."

Outside, thunder spooks all four of us. Bobby clutches a Monopoly box against his chest, shaking. "I think it's an EF5."

Mom sighs, no stranger to this game. "It's not a tornado, baby."

"It might be an EF5."

Dad snarls. "What the hell is an EF5?"

Excitement replaces the terror across Bobby's face. "It's like when two tornados come together . . . "—he drops the Monopoly box and claps his hands together—" . . . and make one giant tornado . . . it *rips everything in its path*." He points to the left, both arms stretched out, stiff, like he's directing a plane to land. "If it goes this way, everything would be destroyed." He gestures the opposite direction. "And everything this way would be destroyed, as well."

"Oh my god," I whisper, heart pounding as I visualize our entire town obliterated. "Is that true?"

"It isn't a tornado," Mom says. "It's just a thunderstorm. Everything's going to be okay."

Dad groans, rubbing the space between his eyes that always seems to be the source of all his pain and frustration. "Bobby, will you stop trying to scare your sister?"

"Or it could be a fire tornado."

I gasp, suddenly feeling flames heating my flesh. "A *fire* tornado?"

Mom reaches out for him, but is unsuccessful. "Bobby—"

"—Like, if you get gallons of gasoline, and you . . ."—he mimics pouring a gasoline canister along the floor—" . . . pour it, and if you want to be all the way over here, you can just pour it more, and you throw a match and the flame would shoot up into the tornado and that would be a fire tornado and everything would catch on fire."

"Are you planning on starting a fire?" Dad asks, sipping from his thermos.

Bobby gives his response serious consideration, then says, "No."

"Then there's not going to be a fire tornado."

Another realization strikes. "Someone else might."

"Someone else like who?"

Bobby shrugs. "I don't know. Just . . . you know, people."

None of this can be real. These alerts are merely exercising caution, something the weather people have to issue or they'll get fined or fired or something. "Mom," I say, "is there really a tornado?"

"No, Mel," she says, voice warm like honey, "there's not a—"

Thunder booms, drowning out any remaining hope.

"That was loud," I whisper, voice cracking.

Mom nods. "It was a little loud."

"A little?"

Dad clears his throat. "Sounded like a gunshot."

"Maybe it's an EF6," Bobby says, then pauses, face all screwed up. "Wait. Is there such a thing as an EF6?"

"I don't know, Bobby," Dad says, chuckling with exhaustion.

"Bobby," Mom says, stern now, "there's not going to be a tornado."

He points at her phone. "Then why is it saying there's going to be one?"

"It's just in case, okay? We only have to sit here a couple more minutes. It's almost over."

Dad smirks into his thermos. "Most things come to an end, don't they?"

"Oh, will you knock it off?" It's amazing, how quickly Mom can transform from soothing parent to bitter spouse. Both of them have practiced this trick to perfection.

Bobby interrupts whatever the hell was about to happen between our parents by snapping his fingers, excited again, like a brand-new idea occurred to him. "Oh! Maybe it's a . . . *water tornado.*"

"Wouldn't that just be a hurricane?" I ask, wondering if he'd asked a doofus question on purpose—anything to extinguish the argument before it got out of hand.

"We're too far away to get a hurricane, sweetie," Mom says.

Despite all his fear, my brother looks disappointed by this answer. "Really?"

"Yes, baby."

He shrugs, never defeated. "It could still be an EF5."

"Okay," Dad says, in no mood to hear us talk, "that's enough, Bobby."

"But I'm just saying—"

"I said knock it off."

Bobby slumps his head, momentarily beaten, then starts shuffling through his board game collection again. "Can we play Exploding Kittens?"

The three of us answer in unison: "No."

"Oh, come on! Please?"

"That game takes too long, baby," Mom said.

"Yeah," I add, "plus, you don't even know how to play."

"I do, too."

"You can't even read."

"*I can read!*"

Dad lets out a growl behind us. It sounds inhuman. "Guys . . ."

"Mom, tell her I can read!"

"Mel, your brother can read."

"*See?* I told you." He sticks his tongue out at me, which I respond with by flipping him off. He gasps. "*Mom did you see what Mel—*"

Dad slams a fist against the sink. "*—ENOUGH—*"

Thunder booms again, rendering us all quiet for a while.

Once, when Bobby was much younger and refusing to eat, Dad grew so frustrated he threw Bobby's plate across the kitchen. It exploded against a cabinet, SpaghettiOs and shards of plastic flying every direction. We all sat at the table, watching him standing in front of the mess he'd created, breathing heavy, reeking of shame. The silence that followed then is similar to the one that follows now.

Mom takes several deep breaths. A fish gulping for water and only swallowing air. "Okay," she says, "why don't we all play Crazy Eights?"

"Not Exploding Kittens?" Bobby says, on the verge of whining again.

"Not right now, honey. But we'll play Crazy Eights, if you want."

"Okay . . ."

I squeeze my fists and dig my nails into my palms until it hurts. I don't want to play any dumb card game. I don't want to be here in this bathroom with my family. I don't want to be trapped here listening to them bicker every couple minutes about things that don't matter. It's not my fault they're unhappy. I didn't tell them to get married. I didn't tell them to have children. If they hate each other so much, they should just kill themselves, do the whole world a favor.

This *sucks*. I need to call Amy. She hasn't responded to any of my text messages since I got home and worry has started consuming me whole. Everything that has happened . . . we can't let these memories exist only in our heads, otherwise we'll go insane, we'll lose our goddamn minds. We need to talk about what happened. We need to have a *discussion*.

I need to know she's okay.

"When can we leave?" I ask, wondering what

would happen if I got up and walked out. Would they try to stop me? *Could* they? Or would they simply allow me to disappear into the storm, swallowed up by lightning?

"Soon," she says, zero confidence in her tone. "I bet, by the time we finish this game, the storm will be mostly done."

"Unless the tornado picks up our house and carries it away," Bobby says.

"Bobby, shut up," I say, not quite believing such a thing could happen, but at this point my mental state is open to just about any possibility.

He sticks his tongue out at me again, the little bastard.

"That only happened in *The Wizard of Oz*," Mom says, trying to calm us down.

"It could happen here, too."

"God," I say, sighing with exaggerated effect, "you are so dumb."

Dad takes a swig from his thermos next to the sink. "Goddammit, what did I tell you about talking to your brother like that?"

"I'm sorry."

"Are you?"

"Let's just play this game, okay?" Mom says.

Dad considers, then shakes his head, disgusted. "I ain't playing shit."

"That's fine. You don't have to play. You do whatever you want to do. Bobby? Mel? Come on."

"Do whatever I want?" He laughs, then keeps laughing, getting louder and louder until he has to double over, nearly spilling the contents of his thermos. "Do whatever I want. *Whatever. I. Want.*"

WE NEED TO DO SOMETHING

He wipes snot from his face with the back of his hand. "Tell me, babe, what is it you think I want to do?"

Mom ignores him and motions for us to join her as he continues laughing.

None of us understand the joke.

We sit on the blanket next to Mom as she shuffles a deck and deals the cards out to each of us. Dad remains leaning against the sink, taking short sips from his thermos, watching our game with absolute disgust. He keeps smacking his lips together. It sounds disgusting. Like something from a swamp discovering life.

Outside, the storm rages on. The rain has gotten so loud we have to shout to make ourselves heard. Wind screams. Every time thunder cracks, we flinch—except for Dad, who no longer seems to care about what's occurring beyond our house. All of his hatred is focused on my mother. This is not a foreign stare, but never before have we all been confined to such limited quarters while rage inhabited him. None of us could possibly guess how he might lash out.

Come to think about it, I can't remember a time all four of us had ever found ourselves in the bathroom together. What reason would we possibly have had, except for tonight's tornado warning? Residential bathrooms like this are built for one person at a time. One door, a shower/tub combo, a toilet, a tiny trash can, a sink and mirror. All of us crammed in here together, the room has never felt so small. The reality of its size burns into my skull. Once sweat locates my skin, it wastes no time in overextending its welcome. There's not even a fucking window in here, which might be a blessing considering the storm outside. My stomach spins in knots as I visualize shards of glass flying across the room and entering my flesh.

"Can you please check the weather again?" Bobby asks, about halfway through our first game.

"In a minute."

"Mom, c'mon, please!"

She sighs, set down her deck of cards, and scoops up her cell phone. She stares at the screen for a moment, without responding, looks at Bobby, back to the phone, then lays it on the floor with the screen facing down. "It says it's almost done."

"Really?"

"Yup. We just have to wait a little bit longer."

Bobby smiles, total relief washing over his pale face. "Whew. I thought it was gonna be an EF5 a second ago."

"Nope. Just a little thunderstorm, baby. Now, are you going to keep playing or not?"

"Yeah," I say. "It's your turn, dummy."

Bobby focuses on the cards. Meanwhile, behind him, Dad pulls out his own phone and concentrates on the screen, then clears his throat. "Weird. The weather app on mine says something completely different."

Bobby whips his head around. "*Is it an EF5?*"

Dad shrugs. "I don't know about that, but it certainly doesn't look good." He licks his lips, enjoying the attention. "There sure is a whole lot of red on the map. Oh, boy . . ."

Bobby gasps, drops the cards, and hugs his knees to his chest, rocking back and forth. "Let me see, let me see, let me see . . . "

Mom casts Dad an ugly stare. "Goddammit, Robert."

"What?"

"You know what."

He smiles. "This is pointless. You think this bathroom's gonna save us if a big ol' tornado comes swooping through? You think it's gonna make any fuckin' difference at all?"

Bobby points at the bathtub. "But Dad! You're supposed to take shelter in a basement during tornados and if you don't have a basement then you're supposed to hide in the bathtub! We don't have a basement so that's what—"

"Bobby, we can't all fit in the tub. And even if we could, there's no point."

"Dad! If a tornado—"

"There's no fucking tornado, Bobby."

"Don't talk to him that way," Mom says, squeezing the cards in her hand hard enough to bend them.

"Oh fuck off. Try telling me how to raise my son again and see what happens."

A long silence follows, everybody too afraid to speak. Dad has never struck me or Bobby, and I don't think he'd ever hit Mom either, but the rate things are spiraling tonight, who knows what's gonna happen? The moment I got home this evening, it felt like he was begging for a fight, it didn't matter with who—anybody would do, as long as they could bleed, as long as they could break.

Eventually Mom says, in the calmest tone possible

given the circumstances, "If you don't want to wait in here with us, you know where the door is."

Dad chuckles. Everything is a joke tonight, until it isn't. "Oh, now I got a choice?"

"I'm done talking to you."

"Finally."

Dad turns toward the door and Bobby freaks out. Like, total panic attack. He springs up and grabs Dad's leg, hysterical. "*Dad no don't go please don't go the tornado there's a tornado—*"

"Bobby, c'mon . . . you're being ridiculous," he says, trying to shake him off.

"*—the tornado's gonna get you please Dad stay here please don't go—*"

Dad sighs, then glances over his shoulder at Mom, smug smile across his face. "You still think I should leave?"

Asking it like a double-sided sword. Meaning something that's a secret, something only the two of them know about. "What's going on?" I ask, receiving an answer in the form of the loudest thunder boom yet.

The bathroom lights blink away from existence and we are consumed by darkness.

Bobby and I both start screaming, which encourages the clouds to do the same. I fumble around for my phone and trigger its flashlight app. All four of us have gone ghost-pale. Bobby hyperventilates in our mother's arms. Dad grips his thermos with both hands, no longer attempting to leave.

"Shh . . . shh," Mom whispers, stroking Bobby's head, "it's going to be okay, it's going to be okay . . . "

I don't know what the hell she's talking about. Things obviously are not okay. Panic eats me up and spits me back out. "Why did the lights go out? What *happened?*"

"C'mon, you guys," Dad says, "it's a *thunderstorm*. Lightning probably hit a transformer or something. Stop freaking out for no reason."

Bobby is still shaking in our mom's arms, feeding into my level of anxiety. "—IT'S A TORNADO IT'S A TORNADO IT'S A TORNADO—"

"Bobby, goddammit—"

A deafening series of thunder cracks ensue.

Followed by a crash loud enough to shatter our bones.

Then our entire house shakes, like we're aboard some sort of amusement park ride.

Outside the bathroom door, something explodes.

Wind howls like wolves hungry for fresh meat.

At this point, all four of us are screaming our lungs off and holding each other—even Dad, whose previous transgressions have momentarily been forgiven, or at the very least forgotten. A stray limb from one of my family members knocks my phone from my grasp and it flies across the room. Its flashlight lands upon our flailing bodies, granting us a target to direct our aimless focus. I stare into it and pray as if it's the light of God, but the only response I receive is more rain.

Outside the bathroom door, the storm's volume intensifies. Rain and wind screech loud enough to drown out the thoughts from our throbbing brains. It is the sound of banshees escaping from hell. When we speak, we are forced to shout and, even then, one cannot be certain of the other's dialogue.

"What happened?" I scream.

"What the hell was that?" Mom says.

"Jesus Christ," Dad says, lips trembling. "I don't know, I don't know . . . "

More thunder.

Dad points at my phone on the floor. "Mel, shine that light over here so I can see."

I hesitate, waiting to see if he'll forget his request. He steps away from us and moves toward the door.

"No!" Bobby cries. "Don't go, Daddy!"

He ignores him and nods at me. "Just get the fucking light, okay?"

Whimpering, I part from my mother and brother and retrieve the phone, then direct its light at my father. He presses his ear against the door, listening for an extended period, then attempts to open it. The door swings forward maybe three inches before coming to a dead stop, banging against something solid on the other side.

The sound of wood hitting wood.

"What the fuck?" he says, trying again, and again.

"What's wrong?" Mom asks.

"It won't fucking open."

"What do you mean, it won't open?"

"I. Mean. It. Won't. Fucking. *Open*," he says, punctuating each word by bashing the door against whatever's blocking it. This progresses into full-on shoulder rams against the frame as he gradually gets more pissed off.

Cold wind and rain blow in through the small opening. Flashes of lightning illuminate the bathroom's depressing interior. The reality of the situation is already sinking in, even if nobody has the courage to voice it yet.

Dad reaches through the crack, feeling around blindly. "What the fuck?"

Mom steps forward, but only barely. "What is it?"

"What the *fuck*?"

"*What?*"

He extends his free arm out toward us and snaps his fingers. "Mel, let me see your phone."

"What? Why?" My body stiffens. Absolutely not. No way.

"Because I told you to."

"I . . . I can hold it."

"Give me the fucking phone, Mel."

Mom sidesteps in front of me, acting as a shield against his wrath. "Don't talk to her that way, you son of a bitch."

"Shut the fuck up," he says, and she deflates. Then, to me: "Mel, let me have the goddamn phone."

At this point I am sobbing and I hate myself for every tear spilled. My father does not deserve a single one of them. Every instinct inside me refuses to relinquish my phone. Things exist on it that nobody else should ever see. Plus, there is the fear that Amy will finally respond while his vision falls upon the screen. The text message conversation we found ourselves in the midst of will not go over well with my father. The context doesn't matter. He will go mad. Mad like insane. Mad like nuts. However, if I continue disobeying his demands, the threat of escalated rage seems inevitable.

I extend my arm out, but my grip refuses to loosen, forcing him to pry it from my grasp. A bizarre satisfaction is gained from witnessing him briefly struggle against my unexpected strength. He takes the phone without another word and points the flashlight at the small opening in the door, face grimacing in confusion.

"What . . . the . . . fuck . . . ?" He sticks the phone through the crack, angling his arm, squinting against the rain. "Oh, goddammit. Oh, motherfucker."

"What is it?" Mom asks, at last triggering the flashlight app on her own phone and directing its illumination upon the door.

"A tree . . . "

"A *what?*"

"I think . . . goddammit . . . "

"Oh my god," I say, no longer able to withstand the suspense. I need my phone back in my possession immediately. "What happened? *What happened?*"

"A tree . . . some fucking *tree* is blocking the door."

"What tree?" Mom says, incredulous.

"How should I know? It's blocking the whole goddamn door."

"You can't move it?"

"Does it look like I can fucking move it?"

"Wait," I say, speaking without thinking, "maybe it's the one in the back yard. Where we buried Spot?"

"*What?*" Bobby screams, snapped out of whatever fantasyland he'd mentally sought shelter in.

"Goddammit, Mel," Mom says.

"I'm sorry!" Despite our current predicament, I feel instant regret for mentioning Spot, who had been our faithful Dalmatian up until about two months ago, when he'd escaped out the front door and crossed paths with an Amazon delivery driver.

"Spot ran away!" Bobby says, having apparently forgotten all about the storm outside. "You said Spot ran away!"

"Shh, baby," our mother says, pulling him against her breast and rubbing his head until he quiets down.

Dad continues pushing at the door, one arm through the crack as he investigates the scene. If a tree has really fallen through the roof, then nothing is in place to prevent rain from entering the house. Everything in my parents' bedroom will be ruined by the time the storm passes. This particular bathroom connects to their bedroom. We have another bathroom in the front of the house reserved for guests and Bobby and I, but that one is somehow even smaller than my parents'. I can't imagine being trapped in the guest bathroom with everybody. I doubt we would have lasted an hour.

He curses something unintelligible and retreats from the door, dripping from the rain that's blown inside our house.

"Where's my phone?" I ask, noticing the absence within seconds.

"Calm the fuck down," he says, trying to catch his breath—but from what?

"*Where's my phone?*" I lose control of my body and begin shaking. I want to shriek loud enough to shatter the universe. "*Where's my phone?*"

"I dropped it, okay?"

Tears run down my face. A mutated croak escapes my lungs.

"I'm sorry. The rain's crazy out there. The wind, it just . . . took it . . . ."

His apology means nothing to me. I fall to my knees and moan, feeling a great pain in my stomach. It is urgent that I speak to Amy. We need to regroup and come up with a plan. We need to fix what we've done. I need her to hold me and tell me everything's going to be fine. I need her to assure me we didn't fuck everything up.

"Oh, would you stop being hysterical?" Dad says, looking down at me with utter repulsion. "It's not the end of the goddamn world."

This last sentence of his is punctuated by an insane series of thunder booms. The sound arrives at a much louder volume with the door slightly cracked open.

Mom asks if we are really stuck.

Dad gestures at me and Bobby, both of us still crying like pathetic little babies. "You think I'd be here listening to this shit if we weren't?"

"Is it . . . ?"

"Is it *what*?"

"Actually . . . you know . . . a tornado?"

"I don't know. The roof's gone."

"Oh my god."

I take several deep breaths before risking speech again. "What do we do?"

"We have to call someone," Mom says.

"Who?" Dad asks, amused.

"Ambulance? Fire truck? I don't know. *Someone*."

Dad leans against the sink, at a loss, sipping from his thermos. He digs out his own phone, dials three numbers, and holds it to his ear. He waits several moments before hanging up and tossing it on the sink. I resist the urge to pick it up and throw it outside in the rain, let him get a taste of his own medicine, see how he likes it.

"Busy," he says.

"*Busy?*" Mom says.

"That's what I said."

"How is it *busy?*"

He shrugs.

"What are we going to do?"

Another shrug. "I guess we wait."

They don't realize I'm already awake, judging by how they're talking to each other. Mom asking Dad how much whiskey he has in his thermos, Dad telling her to get fucked. I've overheard them talking like this before, when they think I'm in my bedroom or somewhere outside. It's gotten worse over the last year, year and a half. When one enters a room, the other typically leaves. Absent are the usual pleasantries most kids expect their parents to share. No *thank yous*, no *how was your day?s*. Most mornings, I wake up and Mom's sleeping on the couch in the living room. Most nights, Dad doesn't get home from the bowling alley until well after midnight, stumbling through the front door reeking of booze, barely able to walk without knocking something over. I can't remember the last time I heard them tell each other *I love you*. Sometimes I wonder if they ever have. It would have been a lie, anyway.

At one point in time, they must have at least *liked* each other. Otherwise, why had they ever gotten together in the first place? Something must've served as the initial attraction. Something must've convinced each other they were meant to be. Whatever that *something* was, it had certainly lied to them.

They couldn't be more different, more . . . the *opposite*.

The way they act around one another, it's less like a marriage, more like an epic rivalry. Maybe that's what all relationships are like. Maybe nobody actually *loves* each other. They just argue and fight and have babies and scream and break things and eventually everybody dies.

The outcome will always be the same, no matter what anybody tries to do.

Everybody dies.

The end.

I think about Amy and refuse to believe we'll face the same fate.

We're better than my parents.

We're stronger.

Goddammit, where *is* she?

I peek around the dark room, double checking the events from last night were real and not some sinister dream. I could have them wide open and still nobody would have noticed I'm awake. Dad has closed the door, so the only light from outside comes from the bottom of the frame. I lie curled up next to Mom across the bathroom from Dad. Bobby snores somewhere between Mom's legs. That kid can sleep through anything.

Dad sets his thermos down, the noise creating a soft ding as it connects with the floor. He turns on his knees and opens the door until it connects with the tree. A thicker sheet of sunlight slips into the bathroom. The rain has stopped. Only the wind makes any noise now. He peers through the crack, studying whatever we can't see, then sighs and settles back against the wall. The door remains open, letting in a breath of cold air.

"How bad is it?" Mom whispers.

"I can see the sky."

"And the tree?"

"Not going anywhere. At least not without machinery."

"Like a crane or something?"

He lets out an exhausted laugh. "I guess. I don't know."

"You think the insurance will cover it?"

Another laugh. "I don't know." He closes his eyes and bangs the back of his head against the wall a couple times. "Almost like this is punishment, ain't it? God's way of reminding you of the vows you made. That he hasn't forgotten and neither should you."

He grins like a real smug asshole. It's how he always grins. It baffles me, how Mom has managed to stay with him all these years. I can't imagine ever marrying a man like Dad, much less allowing someone like him to touch me, or even *talk* to me. Similar types of men exist at my high school. Guys who think they're owed everything just for having a dick. Delusional assholes who think they're the center of the universe.

Barf.

Mom ignores his comments, like she usually does, otherwise she would have probably lost her mind years ago. "You gonna try calling again?"

"Yeah. Okay. Yeah." He reaches up and blindly retrieves his cell phone from atop the sink. He dials the number and raises it to his ear, waits a second, then drops it in his lap. "Maybe something's wrong with my phone."

"Still busy?"

"Try yours."

"I can't."

"You can't?"

She points at her own phone next to her feet. "It died."

"What? How?"

"Flashlight drained it."

"Fuck. You didn't bring a charger?"

"Did *you?*"

"Goddammit." He sighs. "*Goddammit.*"

"The power's out, anyway. Charger wouldn't do much good right now."

He picks up his phone again and starts fiddling with something on the screen, then shakes his head with frustration. "Goddammit, you little motherfucker . . . "

"What?"

"I'm trying to . . . "—he taps the screen furiously—" . . . check the news . . . "—he taps harder—" . . . but this fucking thing . . . "—then slaps the screen—" . . . *isn't working.*"

"How many bars do you have?" Mom asks.

"What? I don't know."

"What does it say at the top of your screen?"

He squints at the phone. "No signal . . . ?"

"Maybe the storm took out a couple cellular towers."

"What do you know about cellular towers?"

"What do *you* know?"

Dad throws his phone back on the sink and it bounces across the porcelain. "This is fucking bullshit."

"Do you want me to look at it?"

"No," he says, sneering, "I don't want you to *look* at it."

"Okay. I was just asking."

I let out an exaggerated yawn, pretending I've just woke up. "Did you get my phone?"

To which Bobby immediately follows up with:

"I have to pee."

Turns out, we all have to use the toilet. Bobby goes first, then Dad, then Mom. They both offer to let me go ahead of them, but I'm trying to prolong the inevitable as much as I can. I've never peed in front of anyone before and fear shyness will freeze my bladder.

During each shift, the other three face the opposite direction, attempting to offer some sense of privacy, as minimal as it seems. When it is finally my turn to sit on the toilet, all I can do is stare at the backs of my family in horror. How had they all managed to relieve themselves with such effortlessness? They'd made it seem so easy, like it was no big deal at all. But it *is* a big deal. People aren't supposed to urinate in front of others, even if they *are* family, even if their backs are facing you. The entire act is unnatural.

"I can't go with you guys here."

Dad laughs. Of course he does. "Well, I don't know what to tell you, Mel."

"We're not watching," Mom says. "It's okay."

"But still . . . you're here. It's too weird."

Mom nods, then leans over the tub and twists the

knob. Water sprays from the faucet, loud and fast. "We can't hear you now!" she shouts over the water.

"Yes I can!" my brother joins in.

I grit my teeth, resisting the urge to strangle him. "Bobby, shut up! Oh my god."

He glances over his shoulder at me and sticks out his tongue. I flip him off just as my bladder surrenders to the bowl. He maintains eye contact the entire time and I've never felt more creeped out in my life. "Mom," I cry out, urine gushing out of me, "make him stop!"

"Bobby, cut it out," Mom says.

"I'm watching you pee, Sis! It's so gross! There's pee everywhere!"

"Mom!"

"Bobby—"

"Drink it, Sis. Drink your pee! *Drrrriiinnk it.* Yum yum yum yum yum."

After I finish up, I punch him on the arm and he starts crying and Dad gets all pissed and spits out this long lecture about how I shouldn't hit my brother, that he's told me how many times not to hit him and do I even listen to a single word he tells me? Do I even care? Of course I don't care, I want to respond, but I'm not suicidal—at least not in this moment of time. Maybe in another hour I'll change my mind.

Later, we sit in a circle on the blanket playing cards. I make a particularly good play guaranteed to screw over Bobby. "Ha. Take that."

His face crumples into an expression of pure horror. "Oh no."

"What?"

"I have to poop."

"Oh no," the three of us say in unison.

It doesn't take long before we're fighting for a chance to press our faces against the door opening, desperate for fresh air, gagging on the hideous stench emitting from my brother's asshole. "Oh god," I moan, "we're gonna die, we're gonna die."

"Jesus, Bobby," Mom says, color draining from her face, "what did you eat?"

"Farts! I ate farts!" he shouts atop the toilet, howling with laughter as waves of flatulence erupt beneath him. "*I ate all the farts!*"

Eventually I have to look outside. *Really* look and take in everything our limited view allows.

Dad hadn't been messing with us. The roof is gone, sliced in half by a tree from our back yard. A tall, thick tree. I don't know what kind. One with bark and branches and leaves. Only old people know types of trees. But it is definitely the one we'd chosen as Spot's final resting grounds. It isn't like our back yard holds a reputation for housing many trees.

The memory remains front and center. Two months ago. If Bobby had been home that day, he would have witnessed the death of his dog. Instead, I was the lucky one who got to watch it happen. Mom and I had gone grocery shopping that afternoon, thinking we'd beat the rush. Mostly our trip had been pleasant, which felt rarer as I aged. Not once did we get into an argument or bring up anything nasty. I think we even laughed together once or twice. Of course, that all changed when Mom opened the front door. Spot must've been waiting for us, planning out his escape all day, just waiting for the perfect moment to make a run for it. Poor little guy. He'd never done anything to anybody. Twenty seconds after he shot through Mom's feet, the Amazon delivery driver obliterated his skeleton. Then he turned into our driveway and, after offering his most sincere apologies, handed over a package addressed to our residence. It was a present for my birthday the following week, I later discovered. A blu-ray of some new Pixar movie. I couldn't have remembered the title if someone pressed a gun against my head. I threw the movie away without bothering to crack the sealing. As far as I was concerned, the entire company of Pixar was now a cursed entity that I would no longer allow to entertain myself. When Dad found out what I'd done with my gift, his face got so red I thought it might pop, and when it didn't, all I could feel was disappointment.

If last night's storm had knocked down a behemoth like this tree, the possibility of what other damage it might have caused around town is enough to snatch my breath away. My parents' bedroom is unrecognizable. The tree blocks the majority of our view, but I can tell their bed has been flipped upside down. Dressers and nightstands rest on their splintered sides. Water from last night's storm drips from the edges of the roof into the soaked carpet below. The sky is blue and clear. Undisturbed. Like everything is perfectly fine and nothing even slightly disastrous has recently occurred.

I wonder what kind of damage has inflicted Amy's house. I wonder if she's okay.

WE NEED TO DO SOMETHING

My cell phone is nowhere in sight.

Another victim claimed by the storm.

I give up and curl in the bathtub. Its cold porcelain feels like a deadly kiss against my cheek. Bobby jolts across the bathroom and takes a turn inspecting the damage.

"Wow. It really *was* an EF5."

Dad nods, leaning against the sink with both hands gripped tightly around his thermos. "Yeah. It might have been."

"Do you think everybody's okay?"

"I don't know."

"I'm sure everybody's fine, baby," Mom says, still sitting against the wall next to the toilet.

"We don't know that," Dad says. "We don't know anything."

Bobby glances over his shoulder, concerned. "Do you think people *died?*"

Mom shakes her head. "No, baby."

"Highly possible," Dad says.

"Goddammit, Robert."

"What? You want me to lie to my son now?"

"No. I just . . . " She shuts her eyes and massages her temple, as if trying to erase her entire marriage through willpower. " . . . I just don't want him to freak out any more than he already has."

Dad gestures at the door. "I think it's a perfectly reasonable time to freak out."

From the bathtub, I emit a guttural moan. "Ugh. When is someone coming to get us?" It doesn't make sense that we're still here. Police exist. Rescue parties. Something.

"The storm is gone," Mom says, and I resist

responding with *no shit*. "Someone will see our house. They'll see . . . what happened to it. Help will come."

Dad clicks his tongue. "Unless every house is like this."

"What do you mean?" I ask, already knowing the answer.

"If the tornado destroyed every house in the neighborhood, or even the town, then it could be a very long time before rescuers make it here."

"Robert—"

"—We could be stuck here for another day or two."

My stomach feels like acid, drip-drip-dripping into my organs. "Oh my god."

"*Really?*" Bobby cries out, a mix of terror and excitement battling each other in his tone.

Mom sighs a familiar sigh. "Goddammit, Robert—"

He holds up his hand like a stop sign. "I'm not saying that's what's gonna happen. I'm just saying . . . we should be prepared to be here a while. It looks bad outside, right? Real bad. I *hope* someone finds us soon, but I'm also trying to be realistic." He smirks at Mom. "Isn't that what you wanted me to be, honey? Realistic?"

She glares at him, refusing to respond.

I can't stay in the bathtub forever. Not with my phone still out there, unattended. Any sort of notification could have been sent to me by now, and there it remains, unread. Surely Amy has responded to my texts. And if she hasn't, then screw my family, I'll call her while in the bathroom where everybody can eavesdrop. Eventually they'll find out the truth, anyway. Things like this, they have a way of coming out one way or the other.

You can't light a fire and expect nobody to get burned.

I sprawl out on my stomach and reach through the door opening. Face pressed tight against the wooden frame, I blindly feel around my parents' bedroom. First my fingers splash in the carpet and I groan. Soggy. Squishy. Flashbacks of Spot leaving puddles of urine throughout the house and everybody stepping in them in the middle of the night, barefoot, barely awake. We tried so hard to potty train that dog, but nothing we did ever seemed to take.

I remember one night, years ago, waking up to Dad screaming his voice hoarse. Normally I stayed in my room when my parents were arguing, too petrified of somehow getting caught in the crossfire, but this night wasn't like other nights. He kept shouting something about a "goddamn dog" followed by heavy, frantic footsteps that shook the whole house. I snuck down the hall and peeked around the corner, into the living room, and found him chasing Spot in a circle. Dad's foot was covered in shit, which he tracked around the living room the longer he tried to catch our dog. Spot was far too fast for Dad, who was obviously drunk off his ass. Eventually he gave up and passed out on the couch and Spot escaped into the safety of my bedroom. I made sure to lock the door before settling back under the covers, giving our Dalmatian plenty of kisses and reassuring him he was, in fact, a Good Boy. I hope he believed me.

I continue my sensual investigation from the wet carpet up to the tree. Its bark is rough and moist, providing a false hope for fragility. I give the tree a shove. It doesn't even do me the common courtesy of pretending to budge. This thing is here to stay, and there's nothing any of us inside this bathroom can do to change that.

I press my face against the opening and peer out again. This time focusing on the carpet, searching for what belongs to me and not finding a goddamn thing.

Where the fuck is my phone?

Five minutes later I give up and sit against the wall next to the door, out of breath and fuming with rage. I glare at my father and try to express with my face how much I hate his guts. He notices, but instead of acting intimidated he just laughs and shrugs.

"Don't look at me like that."

"I can't believe you dropped it."

"It was an accident."

"How are we going to get out of here?"

"I don't know."

"Can't we break the door down?"

"Not with the tree there."

"What about the wall?"

"The wall?"

"What if we busted a hole through it and crawled out?"

"I don't . . . how? With what?"

"Can't you just punch it?"

"No. I can't just punch it."

"It's going to be fine," Mom cuts in. "Everything is going to be fine. It hasn't been that long. Someone is going to come."

"But what if they don't, Mom? What if something happened?"

"Something like *what?*"

Of course I can't tell her about the doomsday scenario entertaining itself in my head. There would be too many questions, and I know the answers to them all.

"Everybody get up," Dad says. "Maybe if we all push at the same time, our combined strength will open this son of a bitch once and for all."

"Even me, Daddy?" Bobby asks.

"I don't know. You think you're strong enough?"

"Hmm." Bobby rubs his chin, thinking it over. "Maybe?"

"Let me see your muscles."

Bobby flexes both arms. Dad gasps in amazement. "Holy shit, son. You got a license to carry those guns?"

Bobby cocks his head, relaxing. "Dad, these aren't guns. They're just my arms."

"Oh." He performs an exaggerated *whew*. "You really fooled me there for a second."

He giggles. "You really thought my arms were guns?"

"Big, giant machine guns."

"Haha. You're so stupid."

Dad glares at him for a second, and Bobby ceases his laughter.

"I'm sorry. I was just kidding."

"Are we going to knock this goddamn door open, or what?" He motions for all of us to rise. "C'mon, get up, let's *do* this."

Eight palms press against the door, our bodies on top and under each other, forming an awkward ball of flesh and sweat. I don't know how long we push, or how many times Dad grunts out, *"C'mon, goddammit,"* at us, but eventually we surrender back to the floor, panting, out of breath. Except for Dad, who remains standing next to the door, staring down at us, not making the slightest attempt to hide his disappointment.

"We're not strong enough," Bobby says. "We don't have enough muscles."

"We could have tried harder," Dad says. "We didn't have to give up so easily."

"Maybe if Sissy's butt didn't smell so bad, Dad. Maybe then we could have kept going."

Everybody turns to me, awaiting an explanation.

"Is this true?" Dad says. "Is the smell of your butt preventing us from opening this door?"

Everybody giggles, including myself. "I hate you all so much," I tell them, still laughing.

I claim the tub as my permanent resting area until this whole ordeal finally finishes. Either help will arrive, or I will die here in this porcelain grave and slowly decompose down its drain. As time passes, I remain uncertain which outcome I prefer most.

On the floor next to the tub Bobby plays cards with himself. Some fake game he's probably made up which consists of several dozen nonsensical rules nobody could possibly understand, including himself. We both look up as Mom rises from the toilet and approaches Dad next to the sink. It's been hours since any of us have actually moved. Or maybe days. Or five minutes. Who knows? Time moves in surreal strides here in this bathroom. Now that our phones are MIA, none of us have any way to tell time. I remember, at one point in time, there being a clock hanging from the wall next to the toilet in our parents' bathroom. Perhaps another casualty of my father's alcoholism. I can easily imagine him coming home in the middle of the night from the bowling alley, stumbling in here to pee, and knocking the clock off the wall with a careless shoulder bump. He probably didn't even notice what he'd done, leaving it for Mom to clean up the following morning. Or maybe it had simply stopped functioning.

Dad's been leaning against the counter, fooling with his cell phone and growing increasingly frustrated with its lack of results. He stops thumbing the screen and acknowledges Mom's sudden closeness with a sneer.

She points at the thermos behind him. "We need that."

Not bothering to follow her gaze, he says, "Need what?"

"It's the only container in here that can hold water. We need to stay hydrated."

"I'm not finished with it yet."

"Well, can you be?"

Dad doesn't react for a moment. His jaw twitches. Contemplating saying something ugly, lashing out, making a horrible time somehow worse. Instead he exhales over-dramatically and chugs the thermos until whatever contents remaining inside disappear down his throat. His face seems to sink into itself as it reacts to such a heavy dose of alcohol, then relaxes a little. He ignores Mom's out-stretched hand and sets the thermos back on the sink, smiling at her, clearly trying to start another argument. Her own expression says everything she needed to say, that she is absolutely disgusted with the man she'd married, that she regrets ever marrying him or having his kids. I do not blame her for this disgust, as I too share similar thoughts.

He chuckles and maneuvers around her toward the toilet, groaning as his knees bend and crack. Mom washes the thermos out under the sink and fills it with water, then brings it down to Bobby and tells him to drink it.

Bobby smells the top of the container and grimaces. "Gross. It smells! It smells just like Sissy's butt!"

"It's okay. I washed it out."

"From the *sink?* But I only like bottled water, Mom!"

"Bobby, does it look like I have any bottled water? If you don't drink this, you're going to get sick. Come on now. Please."

"But Mom—"

Behind them, Dad slaps the wall, startling the rest of us into giving him his full attention. Still seated on the toilet, he starts stomping his feet on the floor like a great beast attacking a city.

"*Bobby,* god*dammit,* drink the *fucking water* and stop acting like a little . . . god . . . damn . . . *baby.*"

Tears had broken through Bobby's ducts before Dad finished screaming. He grabs the thermos from Mom and takes a long chug, trying not to choke on the liquid between sobs. Mom ends up having to pry the thermos away from him after a minute, giving Dad a side-eye of rage and fear, then hands it over to me.

After witnessing my father's tantrum, I do not need any further instructions. I drink the water and try not to gag on the lingering odor of whiskey, then return it to Mom. She gulps the last of it and turns toward the sink to set it back down, but Dad is already up, yanking it from her grasp. He attempts to take a sip, only to realize it's empty. Frowning, he holds the thermos upside down. "So, what, I don't get any now?"

Mom pauses, treading lightly, and gestures at the sink. As if to tell him, *You're a big boy. You can do it yourself.*

The silence between them is sharp enough to puncture flesh.

Then Dad smiles. "Relax. I'm just fucking with you. Jesus Christ. You can't take a joke now, or what?"

He refills the thermos, sips it, then sets it back on the counter, smacking his lips. He starts screwing around with his cell phone again, as if this time it will finally work for some reason. Bobby and I exchange brief eye contact, communicating telepathically the way only siblings can, telling each other that we oughta count ourselves lucky for avoiding what could've been a massive fight between our parents. The longer we stay in this bathroom, the tighter the tension grows. It will not hold forever. Sooner or later, something is going to break.

Something or someone.

Mom suggests we take inventory of the bathroom, which we all agree is a good idea, but none of us get up to help. Instead we sit and watch her go through the medicine cabinet and various drawers below the sink. I don't know where she's found the energy. I barely have enough strength to keep my eyes open. I barely have enough strength to breathe.

She pulls out everything and lines them up along the top of the counter. Once in a while Dad makes snide remarks about the amount of hair products she digs out, stuff like, *"Why do you need all this shit, anyway?"* and *"Good to see my paycheck hasn't been going to waste,"* as if Mom doesn't also work, as if he's the sole provider for this family, which is of course a lie and we all know it, but god help the poor soul brave enough to point it out.

This is what she found:

- Two toothbrushes, along with half a tube of toothpaste;
- Mouth wash;
- Hydrogen peroxide;
- A box of Batman-themed Band-Aids;
- Various hair products (gel, spray, shampoo, conditioner, etc);
- Hair dryer;
- Deodorant;
- Soap (body wash, hand foam, several bars);
- Razors;
- Shaving cream;

WE NEED TO DO SOMETHING

- Beard trimmer;
- Makeup (eye shadow, mascara, eye liner, blush, foundation, lipstick, powder);
- Body lotions (vanilla, baby powder, lavender, coconut, strawberry, rose, black cherry);
- Skin care products (toner, lotion, soap, etc);
- Tampons;
- Pads;
- Alcohol wipes;
- Nail trimmers;
- Ibuprofen;
- and NyQuil.

The last item twists my stomach into a knot. Amy loves NyQuil, says you can trip balls on it if you take just the right dose. Sometimes she tries getting me to do it with her, but I can't stand the smell of it, much less the taste. If Amy was here right now, I would try whatever she wanted me to try. But she's not. I don't know where she is. If she's not also trapped, then why hasn't she come over to check on me? After everything she and I went through, it doesn't make any sense. She would be concerned. She would want to know I'm safe. Just like I'm concerned. Just like I want to know *she's* safe.

And, if not her, then *somebody* should have checked on us by now. We don't live in the middle of nowhere, shut off from society. Plenty of neighbors surround us on either side. Can't they see a tree has crashed through our roof? Can't they see we need *help*?

"Maybe we should try shouting again," I suggest. "Someone might hear us now."

"I don't think anyone's going to hear us, Mel," Dad says.

"No, she's right," Mom says. "We can't just give up. There has to be someone, somewhere. There has to be."

One thing none of us can agree on is how to scream. Either we all stand against the door at the same time and let loose, or we each take turns. Option A) guarantees maximum volume, while option B) promises a stronger longevity. It's impossible to shout for help longer than five minutes, and that's being generous. After so long, you need to rest your lungs. Especially when in poor health, like the four of us. Nobody in this bathroom feels energized. Our muscles are atrophying. Everything is dizzy and confusing and the last thing any of us really wants to do right now is shout.

Mom thinks we should all do it together. Otherwise we're wasting our time. If someone's passing by several blocks from our house, they're not going to hear anything if it's just one person. But four? Then maybe we stand a chance.

I disagree, of course. I tell her we should do it in shifts. It's not like our street's been particularly loud since the storm. We haven't heard any passing traffic, or airplanes, or anything. No people. No animals. I think our voices will carry a lot farther than she's giving us credit. Plus, this way we can scream longer. I tell her the last thing we want to do is waste five minutes shouting our lungs off, only to stop for a rest the moment a potential savior passes by.

Bobby doesn't care which way we decide. He just wants the chance to be loud and crazy.

WE NEED TO DO SOMETHING

Dad, on the other hand, claims to have the "headache from hell" and begs us to be as quiet as possible. No one's coming, he tells us. The only thing shouting will accomplish is pissing him off.

We ignore his pleas and utilize my plan of screaming in shifts. Mom and I let loose with a generic, "Help! Please help! Is anyone out there? Help!" while Bobby chooses to go down a slightly different route by howling like a wolf.

"Bobby, don't be stupid," I tell him. "No one is going to save a wolf. They'll be afraid of getting eaten."

"But I like being a wolf."

"Don't you want to get out of here?"

"Fine, Sis. Fine." He leans against the opening again and continues, this time actually forming words. "Hello! Hello! My sissy farted so much and it smells like broccoli and now we are all gonna die because none of us can breathe! Hello? Hello! My sissy's butt is a monster and we are trapped! Help! Please help save us from my sissy's smelly butt! Oh god! We don't have much time before her butt swallows us up and turns us into big poops!"

This time, when I punch Bobby, Dad doesn't even get upset.

Mom and Bobby are halfway through a new game of cards when he rubs his belly and complains about being hungry.

"Yeah, me too," I say, hating how much I sound

like a baby, but it's true. My stomach feels like it's shrinking into a dark void.

"I know," Mom says, quiet. "I'm sorry."

"How much longer are we gonna be here?" Bobby asks, voice on the edge of whining.

"I don't know, baby."

Now it's my turn to rub my belly. "I wish we had brought some goldfish crackers in with us."

Bobby pretends to retch. "Goldfish crackers are disgusting."

"More for me, then."

"I want some eggs," he says, licking his lips. "I want a thousand eggs—with cheese!"

"Ugh. Only old people like eggs."

"No, they don't. Mom, tell Sis all types of people like eggs."

"Melissa, all types of people like eggs," Mom says, barely paying attention to anything we're saying.

I shake my head. "Nuh-uh. Only old people. And do you know what that makes you?"

"Don't say it." Bobby's expression tightens into ultra-seriousness.

"You know what . . . "

"Mom, tell Sis not to say it."

"Melissa, don't say it."

"Okay." I pause for a good thirty seconds, then shout, "It makes you a tiny old man!"

Bobby slams his deck of cards down. "*Mom!*"

Holding back laughter now, Mom says, "Calm down. It's okay."

"But she called me a . . . "

"—*A tiny old man!*" I shout again, full of glee, and

burst out laughing, which only influences Mom to increase her giggling over on the blanket.

Bobby witnesses this matriarchal betrayal with his jaw dropped, exaggerating offense. For the past year or so, I've found great joy in calling my brother a tiny old man. The joke started one day when I walked in the house and found him sitting on the couch with one leg crossed over his knee, glasses at the tip of his nose, reading a physical newspaper. *What are you doing?* I asked, dumbfounded, and he'd casually responded, *Checking the weather*.

Therefore, he was now forever known as a tiny old man, from that day until the end of time.

"*Fuck!*" our father screams, and all three of our heads spin toward him. He's next to the sink, furiously jabbing the screen on his phone, teeth gritting, veins punctuating against his neck. A second passes and the phone shatters against the wall, pieces of plastic flying every direction. Mom grabs Bobby by the head and ducks closer to the floor, dodging incoming projectiles. I scream out and cover my face with both hands just as a small shard lands in the tub.

Dad loses it. He starts punching the bathroom door over and over, the wood bouncing between his fists and the fallen tree on the other side. "Fucking piece of *shit* stupid fucking battery fucking *useless* asshole technology why the *fuck* do I even pay for this cock*sucking* thing if it doesn't even *do its fucking job!*"

Mom hugs Bobby close to her chest, trying to calm him down, but he keeps sobbing. I notice her still keeping an eye on Dad. Making sure he doesn't get near them. I wonder what she'll do if he starts redirecting his fists upon us. How she will defend Bobby and I. How she will defend herself. Then I wonder what I will do, if I'll find the strength to at least try fighting him off, or if I'll immediately surrender to cowardice and allow the inevitable to unfold.

I curl up into a ball while he continues punching the door, body shaking, eyes squeezed shut, trying my best to drown out the noise of my father punching a door and screaming and my brother crying so loud he doesn't even sound human anymore.

Dad on the floor, flat on his ass, legs curved up into upside-down Vs, back against the door. Streaks of blood stain the wood above him. Both of his hands rest in his lap. He stares at them and we stare at him staring at them. Utter exhaustion befalls his face. His knuckles are black and blue and swollen. If his hands aren't broken, they're still plenty damaged. Every breath we emit is in danger of setting him off again, so for a while we try our best not to breathe. He ignores us and focuses on opening and closing his hand, grimacing with each motion. Eventually the blood on the door drips down into his hair and it's the funniest thing I've ever seen in my life, but it's also the scariest, too.

WE NEED TO DO SOMETHING

Everybody's awake and it's unclear if any of us have actually slept since this whole situation started. Sometimes I blink longer than other times and maybe that's sleep, but who's to say? Definitely don't feel remotely close to *rested*, and judging by how everybody else looks, they don't either. I can't remember the last time any of us changed position, except one of us must've moved at some point, because now Bobby has the thermos again, sipping water and trying his best to avoid eye contact with our father.

"How long have we been here?" I ask, only I don't realize it's me who asked it until Mom looks at me.

"I think this is day three," she says, voice so incredibly weak, and I wonder if I sound the same.

"I thought it was four, maybe."

"I don't know, Mel."

"Why hasn't anybody come yet?"

". . . I don't know."

I know she doesn't know. None of us know. But I have to ask them, I have to say *something,* just to remind myself that the rest of my family exists and I haven't conjured them up with my imagination. Just to remind myself that I'm not alone.

"I don't think it was a tornado that did all this," Dad says.

Mom glares at him, confused, cautious.

And I can't resist the bait. "What do you mean?"

"I think . . . " He licks his lips. " . . . I think something else must've happened. It doesn't make any sense."

"What do you think it was?"

He takes his sweet time forming his theory. So

long, I start thinking maybe he's ignoring me, but then he says, "If it had only been a tornado, then someone would have come by now. We have neighbors. They would've seen the tree." He nods at Mom, smirking. "Your mother would've sent in a SWAT team the moment you didn't return one of her calls." He sighs, knocking the back of his head against the door. "What I'm saying is, it's not like we live in some fucking . . . secluded area far away from civilization, right? This is the suburbs. People call the cops if you drive five miles over the speed limit. Someone should have come by now."

"Why haven't they, Daddy?" Bobby asks, fully alert now.

"Because they're all dead."

He goes wide-eye.

"Robert!" Mom shouts.

Dad holds up a finger and winces at his own swollen knuckles. "Dead, or . . . or they've already been evacuated. Either way, this doesn't bode too well for any of us."

Mom shakes her head at him. "Just because nobody's come yet, that doesn't mean they're all dead, and you know it."

"Something could have killed them."

"The tornado?" Bobby asks.

Dad nods. "Yeah, the tornado, or . . . or something else. Buncha fuckin' towel heads, maybe. Another nine-eleven. Who knows? It could be anything. But we aren't gonna figure it out stuck in here, that's for damn certain."

"Towel heads?" Bobby says, uncertain.

Mom and I exchange uneasy glances. Neither of

us like where this conversation's heading, but what can we possibly do to stop it? Last time he went on one of these rants and I tried asking him not to be such a racist, he called me a liberal snowflake. I didn't even know how to respond to something so stupid, but he was positive he'd won the argument.

Dad nods. "Yeah, towel heads. You know, like terrorists. ISIS. From Iraq . . . the kinda bad guys who did nine-eleven. They teach you about nine-eleven in school yet?"

Bobby shakes his head.

"Goddamn public schools, not even teaching you what it means to be an American."

"What's nine-eleven, Daddy?"

Dad smacks his lips, thinking it over. "Long time ago, before Sissy was even born, these guys, towel heads is what you call 'em, they stole some planes and crashed 'em in these famous buildings in New York. Killed hundreds of people. Maybe even thousands."

Bobby gasps. "Why? Why would they do that?"

"Because they hate Christians, son."

"Are we Christians?"

"You bet your ass we are."

"Okay," Mom says, "I think that's enough."

Dad ignores her. "And maybe something similar to nine-eleven has happened again, only here in Texas, which would make sense, if you really think about it. Most places nowadays, you don't even got *real*, red-white-and-blue Americans, you know? You got these liberal communists preaching socialism kale salads. But Texas? Texas ain't going anywhere. And that scares these terrorists. Makes 'em shake in their sandals."

"They crashed another plane here?"

Dad shrugs. "Impossible to say. But something sure as hell happened. Something bad. Something real bad."

"Oh my god," I whisper, unable to stop myself. "It's not terrorists."

Dad cocks his head toward me. "Then what is it, smartass?"

But of course I can't tell him the truth, despite how bad I want to talk about it, so I keep my mouth shut and roll over in the tub and close my eyes for another sleepless hibernation. The tone in my dad's voice, it's smug enough to make the biggest pacifist in the world commit homicide.

"*Christ I could use a drink,*" Dad's mumbling, repeating the line as he paces the bathroom, running his hands through his hair, eyes crazy, "*Christ I could use a drink, Christ I could use a drink, Christ I could use a drink . . .*"

Bobby and I sit together in the bathtub. He drools on my shoulder, half-asleep. Mom's sprawled out on the floor, next to the tub, and I'm worried Dad's going to step on her. This bathroom isn't wide enough for these kinds of physical activities. But who's going to say anything? The kinda look on his face, I wouldn't dare interrupt him.

" . . . *Christ I could use a drink, Christ I could use a drink . . .*"

None of us can decide how many days have passed

since the tree fell. I don't even have a guess. Several.
Maybe a week? Maybe less. Maybe more. Maybe
much more. Either way, it's been a long goddamn
time since Dad's had any booze, and the withdrawal's
killing him. He can't stop shaking. When he isn't
pacing, he's vomiting water into the toilet. No one will
acknowledge what's happening to him. For the first
time in my life, I wish he *did* have a drink. Maybe then
he would shut the fuck up and stop being such a baby.

" . . . *Christ Christ Christ* . . . "

He pauses in front of the sink and inspects the
numerous objects Mom dug out of the cabinets.

"Yes. *Yes yes yes yes.*"

He uncaps the mouthwash and starts chugging
the bottle. Green liquid trickles down his cheeks and
chin. His Adam's apple convulses as the container
empties. He belches and throws the bottle in the trash
can next to the toilet.

"Yes. *Oh god oh god.* Yes."

He leans over the sink, hands clutching the edge
of the counter, and stares into the mirror. A weird
grin spreads wider and wider across his face.

"Thank you," he whispers. "Thank you thank you
thank you."

I can't look at my dad without feeling physically sick.
If anything remained in my stomach at this point, I'd
vomit all over the bathtub. He's sitting across the
room, back against the semi-opened door, rambling
just to ramble, because he loves the sound of his voice,

loves to think he's so goddamn smart—when, in reality, he's just another moron. Every time he licks his lips I want to grab his tongue and rip it off. I can't believe he lost my phone. I can't believe he would be so *careless*. Except, I should believe it: anything else would have been out of character.

"—remember that movie, the one with Tom Cruise?" Dad's asking us. "*War of the Worlds*, right? Aliens come down in the lightning, they buried these machines in the ground a long time ago, and they start destroying everything in sight. You telling me that couldn't happen? You all heard how loud that storm was last night. You trying to tell—"

"Robert, it's been more than one day," Mom says.

"Wh-what?"

"You said last night."

"You know what I fuckin' meant. Whenever it was. C'mon. It wasn't that long ago."

"Are you sure?"

He starts stammering, struggling to answer, then shakes his head real fast, left to right, right to left. "But don't you think that might make sense? I mean, *something* happened, right? So fuck it. Why not aliens? Why not something from . . . beyond?"

"I saw a video on YouTube about aliens," Bobby says. "It was so scary."

Dad leans forward, genuinely intrigued. "What happened in it?"

"A lady was being asked questions in front of a camera about how one night, a long time ago, aliens came and took her when she was asleep."

"They *took* her?" Dad asks.

Bobby nods. "She woke up on their ship . . . *naked*."

"Why was she naked?"

He glances at me before responding. "They were putting stuff . . . *up her butt*."

"Oh my god," Dad says.

"Why are you looking at *me*?" I ask, horrified.

"You better watch your butt, Sis! Aliens are gonna put *stuff* in it!"

"What do you mean?" Dad says. "What kind of stuff?"

"Like, big machines and cameras and . . . and . . . and stuff. The lady said they were taking all of her memories and learning about humans."

"I knew it," Dad says, rocking back and forth. "Fuckin' aliens. It's fuckin' aliens."

Meanwhile, Mom hasn't stopped giving Bobby a look of complete bafflement. "What . . . what shows have you been watching?"

Bobby shrugs. "I don't know. Shows about butts, I guess."

"That doesn't make any sense," I tell him. "Why would they go through someone's butt to learn their memories?"

"Probably because that's where your brain is, Sis." He grins, forming a new joke in his head. "You have a butt brain, Sis! A butt for a brain! A brain for a butt! And it smells like *poop*. So much *poop*."

Dad slams his hand against the sink counter and we all jump, stricken silent. "Goddammit, Bobby. This isn't fucking *funny*. Are you serious or not? Is that what these aliens did?"

Bobby's lips start quivering. He's trying not to cry. "Y-yes. I'm serious."

Dad's jaw clenches as he shakes his head. "Any goddamn alien tries that kinda shit with me, I'll break their fuckin' necks, and that's a promise. Ain't nobody puttin' nothin' up my ass. Not while I still got a heartbeat, at least." He folds his arms across his chest and inhales deeply before rocking against the door. The rocking has gotten more frequent lately. Plus his hands keep shaking.

I've always wondered if he became an alcoholic before or after he and Mom got married. It's not exactly a question I can ask either of them without receiving an irrational response. If he's always been attached to a bottle, then why did she ever marry him? What could she have possibly seen in him? Nothing about his character has ever seemed even remotely appealing. I've never seen them laugh together. I've never witnessed them engage in a conversation concerning each other's interests. Come to think about it, I don't even know if they *have* interests. Dad goes to the bowling alley and drinks. And Mom? She . . . what? Spends time online? Chatting to people on Facebook like some kinda ancient dinosaur. Who is she always talking to, anyway? It's not like she has any friends—at least, no friends I've ever met.

It's funny. Sitting in the tub now, watching him blubber and make a total fool of himself in the bathroom—it's this same kind of drunken recklessness that drove Amy and I together in the first place.

WE NEED TO DO SOMETHING

I was running late and could hear the school bus pulling up in front of my house. Its engine always sounded ominous, as if promising certain doom, like old bones rattling in a haunted house. Only made it halfway down my driveway before realizing what every head inside the bus was staring at through the windows. At first I thought he was dead, sprawled out in the middle of our front yard, face down in the grass. Instead of fear or dread I felt something more peculiar: hope. Yet, when I approached Dad's unconscious body and discovered he was still breathing, my emotions evolved into a bitter disappointment. Everybody feels bad for the girl who discovers her father dead in the front yard. But the girl who discovers her father passed-out drunk in the front yard? Forget about it. Nobody's ever going to speak to her again.

I kicked him in the ribs. He groaned and rolled over, still out of it. Everybody was watching us. I could feel their eyes like lasers digging into my back. Fuck it, I thought, and stormed the opposite direction. The bus driver waited maybe ten seconds before closing their doors and pulling away. I refused to give any of them the satisfaction of looking back and revealing the tears streaming down my face. I would be the talk of the school for at least the entire day over this incident. *Did you hear about Melli? Her dad's a drunk waste of space, passed out on their front yard. We saw her find him this morning and instead of helping she started stomping on his body before running down the street. Yup. She's a total psycho.*

And they wouldn't be wrong. I *was* a total psycho.

What kind of daughter kicks her own unconscious father in the ribs?

I should have stepped on his face instead.

Fast, frantic footsteps replaced the sound of the bus engine. "*Wait!*" someone shouted behind me. "*Wait up!*"

This time I did turn around, hands tightened into fists, prepared to fight any motherfucker giving me shit. Except, it was Amy. We'd been casual friends by then. Sitting together at lunch. Giggling in class over inside jokes. But we still hadn't talked much about our personal lives. I hadn't confessed the deep shame I felt being my father's daughter. Realizing she'd witnessed my incident nearly made me crumble to ash.

"What are you doing?" I asked, trying not to cry and failing.

She grabbed my hand and it felt so good, I never wanted her to let go. "C'mon, we're taking a personal day."

"What are you talking about?" I'd asked. Truthfully I still planned on attending school. I was just going to walk, take a shortcut, be a little late but nothing too controversial. I'd never ditched a day in my life and the thought of doing so secretly petrified me. And now this very beautiful girl was dragging me away, saying we didn't need school, saying to hell with them all. Did I think of her as beautiful yet? Of course I did. But would I have admitted it?

I don't know.

"Where are we going?" I asked her, and she shrugged, told me she had no idea, did it matter? And, after a moment of consideration, I found it didn't matter. I would have gone anywhere with her.

WE NEED TO DO SOMETHING

That was the day we both experienced our first kiss.

That was the day we fell in love.

All thanks to Dad's alcoholism.

It's weird to think about, but if he'd been sober, I'm not sure any of this would have ever happened.

Would we have still fallen for each other, without first bonding over Dad's front-yard incident?

And, if we hadn't fallen for each other, would I have still agreed to help with the ritual?

But it doesn't matter, because that's what happened.

And now we're stuck here, suffering the consequences.

It's Dad's fault. It's my fault. It's everybody's fault.

We dig our own graves and then we jump headfirst.

Bobby's sprawled out on his back between Mom's legs, head resting on her thigh as she pets his hair. Dad sits on the toilet, elbows digging into his own thighs, face buried in his palms. It's impossible to ascertain whether he's asleep or simply resting. I remain in the bathtub, wishing for the coldness of the porcelain to return. Sweat pours down all four of us and refuses to cease its flow.

"Tell me again," Bobby says.

"Tell you what, baby?" Mom asks.

"You know what. Please."

"Okay. Where would you like me to start?"

"Tell me about how fat you were."

Mom stretches out her hands from her stomach, outlining a pregnant belly. "So fat, if you would have poked my stomach hard enough, it might have exploded."

"Gross!" Bobby says, giggling.

"It looked like I was smuggling a great big watermelon beneath my shirt."

"What's *smuggling* mean?"

"Like it was hiding."

"Like we're hiding in the bathroom?"

"We aren't hiding, baby."

"Oh."

Mom clears her throat and continues the story. "But, instead of a real watermelon, all I had under there was you, and you were begging to come out."

"Was I saying, 'Oh, pretty please, Mommy, please let me out!'?"

I giggle from the bathtub.

Mom smiles. "Yes, exactly like that, and I said, 'Patience, baby, I need you to have patience.'"

"Because you weren't at the hospital yet. You were at Walmart."

"That's right."

"You and Sissy, but Sissy was my age."

"A few years younger, but yes, Sissy was with us."

"What were you buying?"

"A pizza, because—"

"—The meat was frozen!" Bobby says, excited. "The meat was frozen!"

She nods. "I'd laid out a package of hamburger meat earlier that morning to thaw, but after work it was still mostly frozen, so we decided to have pizza for dinner instead."

"Where was Daddy?"

She hesitates, chewing on her lip. "I don't remember."

"Why wasn't Daddy with you?"

"I don't remember, baby."

Bobby turns toward Dad. "Daddy, why weren't you with Mommy and Sissy when I was born?"

He remains motionless on the toilet.

I lean over the tub, unable to prevent myself from whispering, "He was drunk at the bowling alley."

Mom glares at me with icicles for eyes. "Mel . . . not now."

Dad still hasn't moved.

"What happened then, Mommy?" Bobby asks, maybe realizing the potential for disaster if we continue prodding the subject of our father's absence.

"Well, you know what happened," Mom says. "Why don't you tell it?"

"I started kicking you! Real hard and fast!" He pedals his legs out at nothing, demonstrating his expert kicking abilities.

"It felt like a little Bruce Lee was inside me, fighting off a dozen bad guys."

"Who's Bruce Lee?"

"A guy who knows karate."

"Where does he live? Maybe he could help us get free?"

"He's dead, baby."

"Oh." Bobby exhales loudly and rests his feet back on the floor. "I wish I knew karate."

"Well, maybe after this is all over, we can sign you up for lessons."

"Karate lessons?"

"Sure, why not?"

"When are we getting out of here, anyway?"

" . . . I don't know, baby. I don't know," Mom whispers, petting his head and trying not to cry and failing.

At night it's impossible to determine if my eyes are opened or closed. All I see is black. All I hear inside the bathroom is heavy breathing and soft crying. All I hear outside is wind. No animals or anything else with a heartbeat exists. It hasn't rained since the storm. Sometimes I fantasize a flood will pass through our town, into our house, and lift this tree in my parents' bedroom and carry it far away from here. And if it can't do that, maybe it will at least have the common courtesy to drown us.

A strong itch interrupts me from starvation/ meditation. On my arm, under the bandage that's somehow managed to remain attached to my flesh. I rip it off in the dark and let it drop into the unknown. A thick scab welcomes my fingertips like satanic braille. When Amy had cut into it, she hadn't been gentle, not like how I'd been with her own arm. Afterward I had feared it would never stop bleeding.

Now I fear it will never stop healing.

Never stop itching.

I bite my tongue and squeeze my hand into a fist, trying to talk myself out of scratching the source. This one-sided negotiation lasts another minute before I surrender to temptation and dig into the wound.

WE NEED TO DO SOMETHING

Something wet bursts and I don't care, it itches so bad, I can't stop scratching, not for anything. The more I scratch the stronger the itch intensifies. My fingers probe my flesh until they're knuckle-deep and I can't understand why the pain hasn't hit yet. Then I feel something in my wound, something moving. Tiny little legs scuttling against my fingers. I squeeze them and pull it out. An insect of some sort. Hundreds of thin legs. The body's long and thick, like a slug. Slimy with blood or something else, who can tell? I scream but noise refuses to escape my lungs. I try to throw the insect but it clings to my hand. It refuses to let go. *Please stop,* I silently beg it, and after so long only one solution makes sense, so I bring it back up to my arm and push the insect back into the wound. It buries itself into my flesh and disappears. All night long I feel it moving inside me. Eventually I start to welcome the sensation. Then I feel nothing, and all I want in this world is for it to return and keep me company again.

In the morning, I hold my arm next to the door opening and inspect the damage.

The bandage is still on my arm. I peel it off and find the scab, nearly healed at this point.

"What's wrong?" Mom asks.

"I think I'm going crazy," I tell her.

And Dad laughs, sitting on the toilet. "Join the club, baby."

"I used to be a cutter," is the first thing Amy ever tells me, long before the incident with my dad passed out in the front yard. We're sitting side-by-side in ISS—or, in-school suspension. A second ago I was moaning in the bathtub, rubbing my gut, and praying for death. Now I'm where? Back at school? I didn't go anywhere. I can still feel the porcelain against my sweaty flesh, but I can also see Amy next to me at the table. Existing in two different places, two different times, simultaneously. Why am I in ISS? I don't remember. It's not important. What matters is Amy. What matters are her arms. I tried not to stare but she has her sleeves pushed up to her elbows and the farther up her flesh my eyes travel, the more the scars stick out. And she's caught me peeping. A deep shame overwhelms me and I roll over in the bathtub, I look away and try to avoid eye contact, but I can still feel her watching me, waiting to respond. I glance back and her attention has yet to drift elsewhere. If she didn't want this conversation, then she wouldn't have said anything, right? She wouldn't have pushed up her sleeves. Or maybe she was just hot. Maybe I wasn't even on her radar until now, and she's planning to make me pay for my impolite behavior.

Somewhere in another place, another time, Bobby's complaining that he's hungry—so, so hungry—and Mom's saying she knows, everybody's hungry, but there's nothing she can do about it right now, so he's going to have to be a big boy and wait a little longer—and I'm maintaining eye contact with Amy as I ask her, "Why?"

And she smiles when she says, "Because I used to be dead."

I don't know if she's joking or genuine. I don't know if I realize yet that I'm in love. I don't know if we're ever getting out of this bathroom. I don't know where I am. I don't know where Amy is. Are we still meeting for the first time, or has the tree separated us yet? Has the lightning cracked the sky? I don't know what's happening to me. I don't know why I can't stop crying. Mom gives me the thermos and tells me to drink, that we have to stay hydrated, that we have to fight.

"I'm so tired," I whisper, and I don't know if I'm telling this to Amy or my mother or both or no one.

Bobby can't stop laughing. Like, laughing so hard he can barely breathe. Snot shakes from his nose and spills into his mouth and still he laughs. "What's so funny, baby?" Mom asks, concerned. We're all concerned. "Why are you laughing like that?"

"I don't know hahaha," Bobby manages to shout through laughter, "I don't know I don't know hahaha I don't know."

"Well, stop. You're going to hurt yourself."

"I can't help it," he shouts, almost crying now, and doubles over.

Behind us, Dad starts laughing too, almost just as hard.

"What is your problem?" Mom asks him, and he shakes his head.

"I . . . hahaha oh god hahaha oh fuck . . . I don't

know!" Dad throws up his hands, at a loss, and keeps laughing.

Mom shakes her head, confused, then bursts out into a similar fit, and I'm in the bathtub, watching all three of them lose their shit for absolutely no reason.

Drenched with sweat, pale, malnourished, laughing, laughing, laughing.

I open my mouth to tell them to stop it, but instead I start laughing too.

And goddammit, I can't stop.

Oh my god.

I can't.

I really can't.

Sometimes I can't decide what would be worse: if we died from starvation or if we never died.

"Have we always been here?" I ask the room. Anyone who's listening. It doesn't matter who answers.

"What?" Dad says. I don't know where he or anyone else is. I'm flat on my back in the tub, staring at the ceiling.

"You can tell me the truth. It's okay. I can handle it."

"What are you talking about, honey?" Mom asks.

"Have we always been here?"

"What . . . what do you mean?"

"Was I born here? Was Bobby born here? Were we all born here?"

"In . . . the bathroom?"

"Yes."

"No, honey."

I sit up in the tub and glare at my mother, who's standing against the wall clutching her stomach. "You're lying. You're a liar."

"Mel, you're not making any sense."

"We've always been here and you're just playing a trick on us," I tell her. "Admit it. There's nothing outside that door. There's nothing, there's nothing, there's—"

"Hey," Dad says, sternly. I meet his eyes. He's sitting on the toilet again. "Stop it."

"Stop what?"

"Stop talking like a fucking whackjob."

"I'm not talking like a—"

"Yes you are," he says. "You're talking like a fucking whackjob and I want you to stop it right now."

"Okay."

"Yeah, Sis," Bobby says in the tub next to me. "Stop acting like a fucking whackjob."

But Bobby can't possibly be talking, because Bobby's dead. He's a corpse. He reeks of decay. It's just the three of us now. Bobby died. Bobby died and he's not coming back.

No.

That can't be right.

Why would Bobby be dead?

Where am I right now?

"Whackjob," Bobby says again, laughing, "whackjob whackjob whackjob you're a great big fucking whackjob."

I punch him in the arm and tell him he can't use that kind of word and he grins like he's up to no good and, before I can say anything else, he lets rip an epic fart that sends me gagging out of the bathtub.

"Smell it, Sis!" he shouts, intoxicated with evil glee. "Smell my butt! It is your new king! Now worship it, Sis! Worship King Butt! Bow to your fart master!"

Bobby is alive. Of course he's alive.

But am I?

Amy's in the tub, between my legs, back against my breasts. The rest of my family is passed out on the floor. Outside the wind howls like it's alive. I wrap my arms around Amy and she holds my wrists together, sometimes giving them soft kisses, sometimes only caressing them. She's telling me how she used to be dead.

Most people are, she tells me, they just don't realize it.

"What do you mean?" I ask her, keeping my voice low to avoid waking my family.

"They said I was crazy," she explains, matching my whisper, "that I was delusional. I never saw anyone, like, professional. My parents thought I was just acting out. Trying to get attention. I googled what I was feeling. You ever hear of Cotard delusion?"

"What?" The word's foreign to my ears. I lean closer against her back and she smells so good. This is before everything happened. We're in the bathtub but she's not here, not really, she can't be. This conversation, it's in the past.

"*Cotard* delusion," she repeats. "Walking corpse syndrome."

"I don't . . ."

"It's like a mental illness, I guess. People become convinced that they're actually really dead."

"But they're still alive?"

"It's complicated."

"Like . . . what, like zombies?"

Amy giggles and it's the most beautiful sound in the world. "Think of it like this. A long time ago, something happened to me. Something *killed* me. Now inside my body everything's rotting. Well, they *were* rotting, but things are different now. I'm better."

"How were they rotting?"

"I could smell them. Decomposing from the inside out. Nobody believed me."

"So that's why you cut yourself?"

"I guess, maybe, I don't know, thinking back on it, it's all so blurry, you know? If I could still bleed, then I could remind myself that it wasn't real, that I was still alive."

"Did you want to be?"

She stops rubbing my wrists. Her body tightens. "What?"

"When you would cut yourself, what were you hoping to see? Blood or no blood?"

But she doesn't have an answer to that question.

Dad digs out the empty bottle of mouthwash from the trash can and holds it over his mouth, begging for another drop to somehow generate onto his tongue, so desperate he's crying, shaking, crumbling apart before our eyes. "*Please god please god please please please god just one more sip one more sip I swear to Christ all I need is one more sip oh god god oh god please I'll do anything anything you want just one more sip please god please.*" Nobody answers his prayers. He throws the bottle against the wall and pounds his fists against the sides of his head. "Don't look at me like that," he sobs at us, snot and tears spilling down his face, "don't look at me like that don't look at me like that don't look at me like that don't look—"

Dark. Middle of the night. Something's outside the door. Something inside the house. Inside my parent's bedroom. Bobby's the first one to hear it. "*What's that? What's that?*" he whispers, frantic, shaking the rest of us awake. Even he knows to be quiet right now. That whatever's on the other side of the door, it might not be friendly.

We can't see a thing. Communication is translated through hushed monosyllables and shoulder taps. Light footsteps get louder, then stop directly on the opposite side of the door. I can't remember if we left it open before going to sleep. A chilled draft confirms it can't be shut. The unknown being sniffs at the door, smelling us, analyzing our scents. Not a human. It can't be a human. An animal then. Nothing too big. Its footsteps aren't heavy enough to justify a deer.

"I think it's a dog," I whisper.

The sound of my voice excites whatever's at the door. Now it's making more noise. Whining. Pawing at the wood, begging to be let inside.

"A dog?" Bobby says, abandoning any sense of stealth. "*It's a dog it's a dog it's a dog!*"

Although I can't see him, I can certainly hear my brother shoot up from the floor and race toward the door. Dad and Mom both shout for him to stop, to come back, but of course he's not listening. Nothing gets between him and dogs. He would walk through fire if it meant getting to rub a dog's belly afterward.

A soft thud against wood. Bobby leaning against the door. Sticking his hand through? He starts giggling. "It's licking my hand, you guys. It likes me! It *loves* me!" Then, in a hushed voice meant only for the dog: "Who's a good boy? *You* are. *You* are."

I slip out of the tub and tiptoe across the bathroom, joining him on the floor next to the door. "Is it really?" I ask. "How do you know?"

"Touch it," Bobby says. "Here, let me show you." He grabs my hand and guides it through the crack. I feel fur, wet lips, an eager tongue. It whines again. Its nose is cold and snotty. I can't believe it's really a dog.

"What is it?" Mom asks somewhere behind us.

"It's a dog," I tell them, and for the first time since everything happened, I feel a real sense of hope. If a dog can be here, then anything can. A dog means we aren't alone. A dog means we haven't been completely abandoned. A dog means we're going to be okay.

"How did it get here?" Mom asks, voice closer now.

"Well, if the tree cut through the roof, then it definitely collapsed a wall or two," Dad says. "I'm surprised we haven't encountered more wildlife by now, to be honest."

"Do you think it's Spot?" Bobby asks.

No one says anything. Despite the darkness, I can feel all three of us looking at each other, unsure how to respond.

"I think it's Spot," he says again, more confident now.

Weirdly enough, the dog seems to react to the name. It gets more excited, starts licking our hands with an added sense of hunger. Little sharp teeth lightly scrape against me, but not hard enough to puncture skin. Thick layers of slobber web between my fingers and it's so gross but I can't pull away, because what if I never get another chance to pet a dog? The thought is too depressing to entertain. I can't allow this dog to get away. Not right now when we need it the most.

"Spot, is that you, boy?" Bobby says. "It is, isn't it? Everybody said you were buried in the back yard but that isn't true, you just ran away, right? You just ran away, and now you've come back to save us. Who's a good boy? Who's a good boy?"

"*I'm a good boy,*" the dog says from the other side of the door, only it's not a dog at all, not with a voice like that.

In the darkness, everybody loses their shit, including me.

The thing on the other side lets out a deep, guttural laugh, then grabs my wrist tight, preventing me from retreating back into the bathroom. Its tongue runs up and down the back of my hand, then it starts sucking on my fingers, making loud wet disgusting noises that I'll never unhear for the rest of my life.

"I'm a good boy," it croaks, *"I'm a good boy, me, me, me, I'm a good boy, yum yum yum yum . . ."*

I'm screaming so hard it hurts my chest and still the thing won't release my wrist. Bobby's no longer next to me. Did the stranger drag him through the crack? Oh god. Where the fuck is Bobby? No. Bobby's crying somewhere behind me. Hands wrap around my shoulders. My dad. He's dragging me away from the door, shouting, "Let my daughter go, you motherfucker! I'll fucking kill you, goddammit it!" and the threats are only making the thing on the other side laugh louder.

Laughing with my fingers in its mouth.

Sucking hard.

Its teeth press down tougher against my skin and I realize it's going to bite my goddamn fingers off.

Bite them off and swallow them up.

Yum yum yum yum.

"No!" I scream, and instead of pulling back I push forward, fishing around its mouth like a haunted house gimmick. Then I have its tongue in my grasp and I squeeze and pull and it's like I'm wrangling a violent, mutated worm and I don't let go until something snaps and I collapse back against my dad and the thing on the other side of the door lets out an inhuman squeal.

We hear its footsteps, much louder now, as it flees from my parents' bedroom, scrambling up the tree and back into the night.

I can't stop crying as my dad holds me tight and

promises he'll protect me, that nothing bad will happen to me with him here, and for a second I actually believe him.

Then I remember I'm still holding the thing's tongue in my hand, and I freak out all over again.

We don't open the door again until the sun rises. None of us have slept a second since the "dog" incident. Dad peeks through the door opening, searching for the intruder, but whatever confronted us last night is long gone now.

At least, we assume.

A part of me wonders if it's still nearby, waiting.

Watching.

Smelling.

On the other hand, I did claim its tongue, so its likelihood of survival seems slim at this point. We threw it in the sink last night, and that's where we find it now. A pink lump of shriveled muscle. Several hours ago, it had molested my fingers. Now it was dead. I killed it. I won. That . . . that *thing* tried eating me and failed.

"Do you think it was a man?" I ask Dad, who's bent over the sink, inspecting the tongue.

He nods without glancing back. "Some fuckin' creep. He comes back, I'll break his goddamn skull."

"You think he's coming back?" Mom asks. "Don't most things die with their tongue ripped out?"

"What do I look like, Dee, some fuckin' doctor?"

"No. I'm just saying. I think that's a thing people

know. Your tongue gets ripped out, that means you end up bleeding to death."

"Well, let's hope so."

"I see the blood," Bobby says, sitting next to the door with his face pressed against the opening. I stand over him and follow where he's pointing. A trail of blood leads from the door toward the tree, then vanishes.

The same blood that still stains my fingernails, despite how hard I scrub them.

"What are we going to do with it?" Mom asks, nodding toward the sink.

"I don't know," Dad says. "I was just wondering the same thing." He reaches down and pokes it, then recoils with disgust. "Flush it?"

Mom shakes her head. "If it clogs . . . no, that could backfire on us."

"I guess I could just . . . throw it outside?"

"No," I whisper, wondering if I'm actually going to say what I'm thinking, wondering what kind of lunatic would even think something like this. "We can't throw it away."

Dad and Mom give me a look.

"If we don't eat something soon," I tell them, "we're going to die."

Dad laughs. "Mel, you're one sick fuck."

But Mom fails to find the humor. "No. Wait. She's right."

He glares at her. "What are you talking about?"

"Tongues are edible. People eat them all the time. Cow tongues, usually."

"I'm not eating this pervert's tongue."

"We have to, Dad," I say, stepping toward the sink,

suddenly feeling territorial about the tongue. I'm the one who retrieved it, after all. I nudge Dad out of the way and pick it up for everybody to see. A hunter boasting over her big catch.

Is that what I am? A hunter?

A hunter of tongues.

If it keeps us alive, then I'll hunt as many tongues as I can find.

"We have to at least try, right?" I ask. Yesterday, if someone had tried making me eat a severed tongue, I would have vomited in their face.

Mom holds out her hand and I lay the tongue in her palm, paranoid it's going to flop out of our grasp like a fish on dry land. She takes it back to the sink and begins running water over it. "We have to make sure it's clean," she says over the sound of the faucet. "There's no telling what kind of . . . diseases . . . that *man* might have had."

"Mom," Bobby says from the floor, shockingly quiet through this whole conversation, "do I have to eat the tongue, too?"

"Yes, baby," she says, "we all have to."

"Well, that's really gross."

"Would you rather have a mushroom?" I ask him. And he gags. "Ugh. No."

"Then shut up."

Teasing Bobby about mushrooms is a great hobby of mine. He's never had one in his life, but he'll swear up and down they're the most disgusting things in the world.

Mom scoops up her disposable razor from the counter and cracks the plastic casing against the wall, freeing the tiny blade concealed inside. "We'll have to eat it in tiny bites," she says, cutting into the tongue. "It'll be tough to chew, easy to choke on, so we need to be careful."

"You know what," Dad says, "I'm so hungry, I don't even think I'll care. Another day and I'd probably take a chomp out of that creep's dick."

"Robert," Mom says, "don't be disgusting."

"Yeah, Dad," Bobby says, "dicks are for peeing, not eating."

The three of us burst out laughing, then Bobby joins us, pleased with his ability to still amuse his family.

I volunteer to try the tongue first. It was my idea, after all. I'm the one who caught it. Who hunted it. The piece I choose is a small sliver of muscle. It feels gross and slippery between my fingers as I raise it to my mouth and plop it on my own tongue.

A tongue on a tongue.

This close to my face, the smell hits before the taste. I don't stand a chance and begin gagging immediately, but force my lips shut with my palm and keep it inside my mouth, chewing fast and hard, praying for it to be over already. It tastes like old rubber and roadkill. Meanwhile, my family stares at me with utter disgust, like they don't recognize me, and I don't blame them. This is not me. I am not someone who rips out a stranger's tongue, and I am *certainly* not someone who then eats the stranger's tongue.

Yet here we are.

I swallow it, but keep my hand across my mouth for several seconds afterward, making sure I'm not going to puke it back up, then tell my mom to give me another piece.

"Are you sure?" she asks.

I nod furiously. Why else would I have asked for another if I wasn't sure? "Yes. All of you. Eat. We have to eat."

"What does it taste like?" Dad asks.

"What do you think?"

He laughs. "Goddammit, this is going to suck."

"Eat it, Daddy!" Bobby shouts, giggling. "Eat the tongue!"

Then Dad hands him a slice of it and Bobby falls silent. "You too, buddy. Dig in."

"Do I gotta?"

"Yes."

"I don't—"

"Bobby. Eat it. Now."

Less than a minute later, he's vomiting into the toilet.

Another thirty seconds pass, and Mom and Dad join him.

Somehow, I'm the only one who manages to keep it in my stomach. Over half of the tongue remains on the sink, which Dad picks up and hurls through the door opening. "It's no good," he says, moaning and clutching his gut, "no good, no good, no good . . . "

A day passes. Maybe several days pass. We blink a lot. We cry. We piss and shit while avoiding eye contact. I think we sleep. My eyes burn. Every muscle aches. A gnawing throb digs into my cranium any time I try to process complex thoughts. I'm so hungry I can't stand it. I would kill for another tongue. I would eat tongues every day if I could.

Tongues. This whole thing started with a tongue, didn't it? Not just one, either. Of course not. A world plagued by tongues, flapping like meaty perpetual motion machines. First with Amy's tongue, inside my mouth, then my own, inside hers, both of our tongues swirling together in a forbidden dance. The best dance. One I prayed would last forever. And maybe, if it'd ended there, we'd be okay, we wouldn't be trapped in this goddamn bathroom, the world wouldn't be ending. But what happened?

"You know what happened," Amy says, not inside my head but inside the bathroom again. We're lying together in the tub, face-to-face, limbs wrapped around each other like we're one being, one creation. An aerial viewer would find it impossible to determine where one of us began and the other ended. Her breath smells rancid but I don't care. If worms burst from her mouth I would greedily slurp them down my own throat and ask for seconds. Nothing that belonged to her would ever be repulsive in my eyes. Anything less would make her somebody else. Anything less and she wouldn't be the girl I loved.

The girl I *love*.

"You know exactly what happened," she says again, voice low enough not to draw attention from the rest of my family. They're all asleep, anyway, snores rasping out of them like death rattles. Soon the noises will be the real deal and Amy and I will be able to speak as loud as we want. Soon nothing will matter.

"Joe," I whisper. Uttering the name aloud is

enough to make me gag. *Joe, Joe, Joe . . .* you little shit. None of this would have happened if you hadn't ruined everything. "He caught us, at school."

Amy nods. "My hand was down your pants . . . and that fuckin' automatic flusher kept going off . . . "

We share a little giggle.

"What was he even doing in the girls' bathroom?"

"Following me." Amy hesitates. "I think he was already suspicious."

"He loved you."

"Was obsessed with me."

"Used to follow you in the halls, try sitting next to you in class. It was creepy."

"Remember the notes he'd leave on my desk?"

"Why wouldn't he just take the hint? Why couldn't he understand you weren't interested?"

"It didn't matter what I felt," she says. "Guys like Joe—once they want something, they won't rest until they have it."

Joe was a loner. He had fewer friends than I did. Not because he was weird or a nerd or anything like that. Simply put, Joe was an asshole. Everybody saw through him. The kinda guy who thought he was better than anybody, and wasn't shy about letting it be known. Nobody wanted to hang out with him because his presence was unbearable. Of course, from his perspective it was everybody else who were the assholes. Nobody understood his genius. Fucking whatever. Joe sucked and we all knew it.

"In retrospect," Amy says, "we shouldn't have been surprised at what he did. It was a total Joe thing for him to do."

"No." I shake my head and hold her tighter,

wanting to tell her there was no excuse for his actions but struggling to form the right words.

She smiles and kisses my cheek. "You don't need to say anything. Anything you think, I think."

"How?" I ask. So tired. So very tired.

"We are one."

"I don't understand what's happening."

"No one's asking you to."

"When the video started spreading at school, and I saw you were in it, and I saw what you were doing, I knew right away it wasn't you. I knew he had done something to make it look like you. I ran through the school wanting to kill him."

"Would you have, if you'd caught him?" Amy asks.

"Kind of a dumb question now, don't you think?"

"How did you know it wasn't me?"

"What?"

"You said you knew right away. How?"

"Easy," I tell her. "The girl in the video, she was naked."

"Yes . . . ?"

"She didn't have any scars."

"Oh."

I'd never heard of deepfakes until Amy explained them to me after everything calmed down. Basically, you take dozens (or hundreds) of photos of someone's head, upload them into an algorithm for like twenty-four straight hours, then you're able to replace the head of a person in a pre-existing video with the head you uploaded. Internet dickheads do it a lot to troll people they hate. Make it look like their "enemies" are having sex on camera. "Revenge porn is big with these nerds," she told me after school that day. I'd come running to her house in tears and she'd met me at the front door, took me around back to the tire swing behind their garage.

"That's what this is?" I asked her. "Revenge porn?"

And she nodded. "He uploaded it on all the major sites. Emailed everybody at school. They think it's me."

"But it's *not*."

"You know that doesn't matter."

"We have to do something," I said. "We can't let him get away with this."

Back in the bathtub, Amy nods. "And we did do something, didn't we?"

"We took it too far," I whisper. "Everything just kept getting worse."

"Do you want me to apologize?"

"No," I tell her. "Please. Never apologize."

She laughs. "Motherfuckin' tongues."

And I return the laugh with one of my own. "Motherfuckin' tongues."

"I guess, in retrospect, substituting had been a bad idea."

It isn't like we were left with much choice. The spell called for a beef tongue and we'd *tried* to obtain one. What we hadn't expected was how expensive they'd end up being. The cheapest one we found locally cost over twenty dollars. And, since butchers typically did not accept Hot Topic and iTunes gift cards as valid currency, that left us shit out of luck.

And who knows? That could have been the end of it, right? Except I couldn't let things rest. Joe had to fucking pay. I started thinking about Spot, still fresh in the grave in our back yard. The Amazon delivery incident had only occurred a couple weeks ago at that point. It wouldn't cost a dime to dig him back up. Why would anybody notice? It'd be easy. And it was. That very night, I snuck out with a shovel, spent fifteen-to-twenty minutes unearthing the ground. We hadn't even stuck Spot in a box. Just chucked him in, unprotected, for the insects to feast. A much bigger challenge followed, however. Prying open his mouth and pulling out his tongue far enough to cut it off. Doing all of this without puking in his tiny grave. I kept expecting Spot's corpse to suddenly lash out and bite my fingers. I would have deserved it.

The next day, I got up early and met Amy at her house. By then we were skipping school like it was a hobby.

"Who needs school?" Amy asks in the bathtub. "Anything you want to know can be found on the internet."

"Like spells?" I respond, a little snide maybe.

"I wonder how grumpy all those old magicians would get if they discovered one day their secret grimoires would be uploaded as PDFs for the whole world to look at whenever they wanted."

"Probably pretty grumpy."

"Oh well," she says. "They're dead now, anyway."

"Aren't we all?" I ask her.

She ignores me and kisses my cheek again. "When you brought me the dog's tongue, I couldn't believe it."

"You didn't think I would do it?"

"I don't know. Maybe I was hoping you wouldn't."

"Why?"

"You never get a bad feeling for absolutely no reason?"

The spell was simple, Amy assured me. People did it all the time, especially the mob. *The mob?* I'd shouted in her empty house. And she nodded, explained sometimes people tried testifying against them in court, so what did they do? Performed a beef tongue spell on the witness. Real bona fide hoodoo. Suddenly the witness no longer wants to testify. What this spell does, she told me, is convince people to stop talking shit about you. It gives them a stern warning that you aren't someone to be fucked with, *or else*.

"So," she said, taking the plastic bag holding Spot's tongue, "let's give this motherfucker a warning, shall we?"

Trying to remember the ritual now gives me a headache, or maybe I already had a headache. Starvation is rotting me from the inside out. "You had the supplies ready," I tell Amy in the bathtub.

"I'm a collector. It's what I do."

"A collector of what?" I ask her.

But she only grins, then sticks her tongue out and licks the tip of my nose.

I stood aside and watched her get to work, like she'd performed the spell a thousand times before. Slitting open Spot's tongue lengthwise and setting it on a glass saucer. "Back to you in a second," she'd told the tongue, as if it were still alive, as if it could hear her. Then, on a small piece of brown paper, she wrote Joe's name three times in a stacked column. After rotating the paper counterclockwise, she then scribbled *SHUT THE FUCK UP* across each use of his name.

"I remember you asking me if I was sure it was going to work," Amy says, lips next to my ear in the bathtub. "Wasn't it fun, back when there was still room to doubt each other?"

"I never doubted you."

"But you could have."

"The stuff you dabbed on the paper. The one you wrote Joe's name on. What was it?"

"Shut the fuck up oil," Amy says.

"Ha ha."

"I'm serious."

"You made it?"

"From a recipe I found online. Slippery tongue, deerstongue, nettle, sassafras, and . . . bloodroot, I think."

"Where the hell did you even get all that?"

"I told you. I'm a collector."

"I didn't know you were so good with needles, either. The way you sewed the paper into Spot's tongue, it was all very neat and professional."

"Aww, thank you, baby."

Sewn it, yes, but also tied the remaining black thread around the tongue like one would restrain a prisoner. Then she carved Joe's name into a black candle, along with *SHUT YOUR FUCKING MOUTH*, and dug it into the tongue, using its rotted meat as a makeshift base.

She dumped the rest of the shut the fuck up oil on the tongue.

After she lit the wick, she had me sit across from her, and together we prayed over the flame, reciting words that made sense in the moment but no longer sound intelligible here in my parents' bathroom. The wax melted down the candle, sizzling against the tongue and conjuring a grotesque scent of decay.

Once the candle was finally spent, she dropped the congealed tongue into a glass jar of vinegar. This way, she explained, anything Joe tried saying about her would be turned against him. *This is how we really make him suffer*.

The next day at school, our homeroom teacher informed the classroom Joe had passed away in his sleep. She didn't specify how, but I already knew the truth.

"He choked to death on his own tongue," I whisper in the bathtub, holding Amy so tight I'm afraid she might break.

"He got exactly what he deserved," she tells me.

"Is that what we're getting now?" I ask her. "Exactly what we deserve?"

Her response arrives with zero hesitation: "Yes."

In the bathtub, I close my eyes and when I open them, Dad has materialized in the center of the bathroom, staring down at Bobby, who's sleeping flat on his back. Dad nudges Bobby's ribs with his foot and he stirs away, gasping at the sight of our father above him.

"D-D-Daddy?"

"Get up."

"Why?"

"When I tell you to do something, do you do it or do you question me?"

"I do it."

"Then do it."

WE NEED TO DO SOMETHING

Bobby slowly stands, eyeing Mom across the bathroom, who's just woken from all the commotion.

"What are you looking at her for?" Dad says, tapping him hard on the back of the head. "I'm the one talking to you, right? Look at me."

Bobby looks at him, tears in his eyes.

"What's going on, Robert?" Mom says. I don't utter a word, praying they forget I exist for the time being. It seems to work.

"Bobby and I are gonna try something."

"Try what?"

"Calm the fuck down." He sneers back down at Bobby and says, "Come on," then leads him to the semi-open bathroom door. He waves at the gap with one of his injured hands. "You see that?"

"See what?" Bobby asks.

"The goddamn opening. Do you see it?"

"Ye-yes."

"I need you to go through it."

Bobby glances up at him, incredulous. "Wh-what?"

"If anyone's gonna fit through it, it's gonna be you. C'mon now."

"I . . . I can't."

"You haven't even tried. Can't you at least try? What's it gonna hurt to just try?"

Bobby attempts to look around Dad to our mother, but he reaches out with a discolored hand and guides Bobby's jaw so they're maintaining eye contact.

"Why do you keep looking at her, huh?"

"I don't know."

"I'm your daddy, right?"

83

Bobby doesn't say anything.

Dad clenches his jaw. "*Right?*"

"Yes."

"And don't you trust your daddy?"

"I guess."

"You guess?"

"I don't know."

"You don't know if you trust me?"

"Yes. I trust you."

"And you want to make me and your mommy happy, right?"

"Yes."

"Then you need to help us get out of here." He gestures to the opening again. "You need to squeeze through." His voice lowers into a whisper. "*Please.*"

Mom leans forward. "Robert . . ."

Dad grits his teeth and says, "Shut up," then, back to Bobby, "C'mon now, boy. You can do it. I believe in you. *Do it.*"

Bobby hesitates several more seconds, and I'm debating trying to put an end to this, but a part of me is also curious to see if he can actually squeeze through the door. My brother isn't the tiniest little boy on the planet, but he sure isn't the biggest, either. Him making it to the other side may sound unlikely, but it's far from impossible.

He steps forward, closing in on the crack between door and doorframe, and stretches his arm through it, then his leg. His foot and calf manage to make it through, but his thigh gets lodged between the wood. He pauses and glances back at our father.

"I'm too big."

"You aren't even trying."

"But . . . "

"You can fit. I know you can fit. You *have* to fit, okay? So just quit being a baby and . . . and just fucking *do it*, okay? *Okay?*"

"Okay . . . "

I don't understand why Mom hasn't put an end to this. She's sitting on the floor, watching them, and I'm doing the same. Then I realize she hasn't done anything because she's also waiting to see if it works, hoping he can fit through and get help. It doesn't matter if Dad's being an asshole about it. *Someone* needs to escape. It only makes sense to start with the smallest in the family.

Bobby presses his head against the opening and attempts to squeeze through. Little success is reached. He groans and continues pushing. Nothing happens. He gives up and starts retreating when Dad grabs the back of his head and pushes it harder into the opening. Cramming my brother's skull through like expired meat into a garbage disposal. Only a small diameter of his forehead makes it through. Bobby's limbs start writhing and flailing as he screams, helpless.

"*C'mon*, goddammit, *squeeze*, you can do it, fucking *squeeze* . . . "

Bobby's screaming louder now, trying his best to fit through the opening, but there's no way in hell any child, no matter the size, is going to fit. It's simply not wide enough.

Mom snaps out of her daze and springs to her feet. She leaps on Dad's back and wrestles him away from the door, long enough for Bobby to flee to the bathtub where I've been hiding this whole time, equally petrified. I wrap my arms around my brother and hug him close to my body. Dad flings Mom off and she goes sprawling across the floor and everybody's crying now except for Dad. He towers above us, breathing heavy, studying our tears. A mixture of emotion drains from his face, from total rage to shock to confusion to slow understanding to, finally, depression. He backs against the door then lowers himself to the floor, defeated.

Several hours of silence later, he whispers, "I'm sorry."

All four of us gather in a circle on the floor to play a game of Mexican train dominoes. We used to play this all the time when I was younger. We used to do a lot of things as a family. Like eat at the kitchen table. Watch shows. Go on walks around the neighborhood. Back when Spot was still alive, we'd all take him down to the park and get him to chase a tennis ball. But then Spot died. Then Dad started working more hours and spending more time at the bowling alley. If I stayed home, some kind of argument was bound to ensue, so I found myself spending more and more time at Amy's house whenever possible. Maybe that's what happened to everybody. Nothing lasts forever. One day you're playing Mexican train dominoes with your family and the next day you haven't spoken to your parents in a week besides the obligatory *good morning* and *see ya later*.

Until the day came when you were trapped in a

bathroom with them all, and nobody came to save you, and slowly you rotted away to nothing until you finally deteriorated from existence.

"How much longer can we survive like this?"

Silence.

Mom and Dad exchanging glances.

Mom clears her throat. "It's hard to tell, honey."

Dad nods along with her. "The one thing that's on our side right now, that we have to remain grateful for, is we have a steady supply of water. I think we can survive a couple weeks without food. But if we didn't have water? I don't even think we would have made it this long."

Bobby gasps, the realization hitting him for the first time. "Are we going to die?"

Mom shakes her head and caresses his cheek. "No, baby. Nobody's gonna die."

"As long as we play it smart and don't act like dumbasses," Dad says. "Anybody can survive anything, assuming they handle it the right way."

"Are we handling it the right way?" Bobby asks.

Dad holds up the thermos. "We're staying hydrated, and that's the most important thing right now."

"But it's making me have to go pee soooo much!"

The three of us giggle.

"It's a good thing we still have a toilet, huh?" Mom says.

Bobby grins. "Yeah, and you have to all watch me shake my booty as I pee!"

"You're disgusting," I tell him.

Bobby sticks out his tongue.

I flip him off.

"I'm sorry if I've been . . . well, you know. Upset. Out of control." Dad licks his lips as he struggles to figure out his apology. I can count on one hand how many times I've ever heard my father apologize. He must have really realized he's gone out of line here. His body looks weak, fragile. All the fight's drained out of him. "I guess I'm just scared, just like the rest of you, and I know that's no excuse for the way I've been acting. I should be stronger for my family. For my children." He glares at Mom. "For my wife."

"It's okay," I whisper. I don't know if I actually think it's okay, or if I'm just telling him what he needs to hear. His words are sincere. I've often considered his rage to mimic a demonic possession; how he's able to flip from perfectly nice and caring husband and father to something far more sinister and terrifying. Like right now. How long has it been since he called me a spoiled fucking brat? Now there are tears in his eyes, and looking at them generate some in my own.

Everyone in this bathroom is wondering the same thing. We're all asking each other the same questions. *Are we doomed? What is happening out there? Are we going to die?* Questions with answers just out of grasp, like a prisoner jailed inches from the key to his cell.

Sit in the same room with someone long enough, and you quickly realize there's only a finite amount of conversation starters. Especially when it's with your immediate family, people you've lived your entire life with. We talk about TV shows and movies coming out soon that we're excited to watch, as if there's any fucking hope we'll ever actually get to watch them. Life as we know it has dramatically changed, and the likelihood of a return to normalcy seems slim to none.

This current round of Mexican train dominoes comes to an end, and we all count up our hands and announce our scores aloud.

"Why are we even counting? Nobody's keeping track," I say. "Especially since *soommmebody* forgot the pen and paper . . . "

Bobby sighs. "I told you I was sorry!"

"I'm getting bored of this game, anyway."

"I'm getting bored of your face," Bobby says.

"Well, what else would you like to play?" Mom asks.

I pause, thinking it over, then throw up my hands. "We've played everything a thousand times already."

"I know. I'm sorry."

"We can keep playing Mexican train dominoes," Bobby says. "I think I'm winning."

"You can't even count up your own score," I tell him.

"I'm winning and you're losing! You're *losing,* Sis. You're losing!"

I shake my head at him. No way am I lowering myself to respond to such immaturity. "I wish we could watch TV."

"Yeah! I want to watch TV, too!"

"Is it Tuesday yet?"

Silence.

"I think it's past Tuesday," Dad says.

"What day is it?" Bobby asks.

"I . . . I don't know."

I lean back against the bathtub, exhausted but tired of sleeping. "The last episode of *The Nightly Disease* was supposed to come out on Tuesday."

"I'm sure it'll still be on Hulu when this is over," Mom says.

"What if it's never over?" I ask, which is the question we're all wondering but I'm the only one with enough courage to actually say it.

"We can't talk like that," Mom whispers.

"Why not?"

"We just can't."

"We might never watch TV again."

"Shut up! Stop lying!" Bobby shouts, then to Mom: "Is she lying?"

Dad rubs his temple and says, "Everybody needs to lower their voices right now."

My body tenses and I'm positive Mom and Bobby's do the same. We stay quiet for all of thirty seconds before the urge to speak overwhelms me.

"I can't believe the hotel show is really over," I say. "We've been watching that for so long. Since Bobby was just a little baby."

"I was never a baby!"

"Shut up, Bobby."

"You're the one who has always been the baby."

Ignoring him, I ask the room how they all think it ended.

"What?" Mom says.

"The hotel show. What do you think happened in the last episode?"

"We'll find out soon," she says, sounding like she's a million miles away.

"I know," I say, frustrated, "but if you had to guess . . ."

"Oh, I don't know. What do you think?"

I smile, because obviously I've been waiting patiently for someone to be the one to ask me this question all along. "Kia better come back to the hotel.

Her and Isaac are meant to be together, right? Maybe they'll get married and run away and never have to work again."

Bobby grimaces. "That's disgusting, Sis."

"No, it isn't. It's romantic."

"Your big fat butt is romantic."

"Shut up, Bobby. Like you know how the show's gonna end."

"I do, too."

"You don't even pay attention when we watch it."

"Yes I do!" He turns to our mother. "Mom, tell Sissy I pay attention!"

"Then how did it end, smarty pants?" I ask.

Bobby bites his lip, concentrating. "I think, maaaaaybe . . . they all farted so much that they died."

"I hate you so much."

Bobby rolls on the floor, laughing himself silly.

I ignore his outburst and ask Mom what she thinks.

She snaps out of some daze and goes, "Huh?"

"The hotel show."

"Oh, yes." She pauses, nearly nodding off, then jolts awake a little. "Maybe . . . I don't know . . . maybe he'll finally quit and find a new job. Something that makes him truly happy."

Dad lets out an abrupt laugh, and everybody looks at him, startled. "A little on the nose there, don't you think?" he says to Mom.

"I don't know what you're talking about."

Dad licks his lips, grinning. "Okay, sure." He glances at me. "You want to know how this show is gonna end? I'll tell you. This guy, Isaac, he's never going to escape the hotel. He'll be stuck there the rest of his miserable life. Nobody will ever come to help him. He will die in that hotel. And that bulimic bitch, what's her name—?"

"—Kia."

He nods. "Yeah, *Kia*. Maybe she'll come back, like you said, but only to manipulate Isaac into giving her money or breakfast or a place to stay. But she never loved him, and she never will. Fat fucking chance. Nah. What's really going on, I bet you anything, is that she already has someone else she's been seeing, some little fucking asshole who's benefiting from all of Isaac's . . . generosity. And in the last episode? Isaac finds out that Kia's been using him all this time. Maybe he's a coward and does nothing, or maybe he actually grows some balls, slaughters both her and this other guy in the lobby, teaches them both a lesson. That's how the show ends. That's how it was always going to end."

A long silence follows as Dad catches his breath. We're still sitting in a circle, surrounding lines of dominos but nobody's really into the game anymore. We're all staring at Dad, horrified. Meanwhile, he's smiling like he just told the funniest goddamn joke in the world.

Before any of us can respond, we're interrupted by a loud, frantic voice from outside.

Outside.

"Hello? *Hello?* Please god somebody fucking *help* me! Please!"

All four of us look at the door, then at each other, then the door again, the whole time this guy doesn't stop screaming for help. We allow another second to pass then scramble off the floor and rush toward the door. Dad forces his face against the crack, trying to locate the source of the voice.

"Who's there?" Dad shouts into the opening. "We're over here. Hey! We're over here! *We're over here goddammit!*"

"Do you see someone?" Mom asks. "Who is it?"

"I can't see shit," he whispers, then starts shouting again. "Hey! Can you hear me? We're over here!"

"Where are you?" the stranger shouts back. "I don't see you. Follow my voice! I need help. *Help.*"

"We can't!" Dad responds. "We're stuck. You follow *my* voice."

Now we're all shouting at the man, screaming for him to follow our voice, for him to rescue us, until—

"I need help, goddammit!" screams the stranger. "I need—" His voice starts stammering, then lowers in volume. "Oh uh uh uh uh no no no no it's not what, oh god, not now, please, don't don't don't don't don't *DON'T—*"

"—what the fuck are you—"

Loud machine gun fire interrupts all other noise.

We jump back from the door, bodies trembling. Suddenly it's very difficult to continue standing, my legs are shaking so bad.

The stranger's screams cease.

Hesitating, Dad steps forward again and peeks through the crack.

"Do you . . . do you see anything?" Mom asks, several feet away from the door.

Dad backs away, shaking his head. "No. I don't see anything. But . . . but I think we should close this for a while."

Nobody argues.

He reaches forward and slowly shuts the door, showering us in darkness save for the faint light beneath the wood.

"What—what—what happened?" Bobby asks, choking on his own tears.

"Shh," Dad says. "Be quiet."

"No talking right now—okay, baby?" Mom says.

"Shut the fuck up. All of you."

Dad pushes the door open, cautious, peeking through the crack, then backs away and leans against the sink. Light illuminates more of the bathroom. The rest of us sit in the tub together. Bobby has fallen asleep. Mom and I look like we haven't slept in weeks. Dad looks like he's never slept a day in his life. We're all pale and ready to die. My stomach's a raw void eager to swallow me whole and I grant it permission without hesitation.

"Okay," Dad whispers, "I think it's safe to talk now, but let's still watch our volume . . . just in case."

"Just in case of what?" I ask.

" . . . I don't know."

"What did you see out there?" Mom says.

"I couldn't see shit."

"Did someone shoot that guy?"

Dad goes wide-eyed and psychotic. "I'll fucking kill them all, I swear to fucking god."

"Maybe he was shooting something," I say.

"*Something?*" Dad says, curious.

"I don't know."

"Like that dog!" Bobby says. "The dog that wasn't a dog."

"Your sister killed it."

"How do we know?"

"I just know."

"What was it, if it wasn't a dog?"

"Bobby, do I look like I fuckin' know?"

"It could still be alive," he says. "It could have grown a new tongue. It could have attacked that man."

"It could have been anything," Mom says.

"Then why did he stop talking?" Dad says. "Why haven't we heard from him since the shooting?"

"I don't know."

"I'm scared," I whisper.

"Me too, honey."

Dad rubs his hands through sweaty hair, gritting his teeth. "God, this is so fucked."

"What are we going to do?" I ask.

Nobody answers.

I clear my throat and ask again. "What are we going—"

Dad bursts out laughing. "Why the fuck do you think *we* have any answers, Mel? We know just as much as you do. Which is fucking nothing, okay? *Okay?*"

"Okay."

"Robert," Mom says. "Come on."

Dad doesn't say anything for a moment, like he's trying to control his temper. "Okay. I'm sorry. I don't know what we're going to do. I don't know what's outside. I don't know who shot who or why they shot them. I don't know if we're ever going to get out of this bathroom to find out. I don't know if I even *want* to find out. I don't know a goddamn thing about anything right now."

Bobby has the right idea. I can't stop thinking about the thing we mistook for a dog however many nights ago. Last night? Last week? What the fuck. What the *fuck*. I don't *know*. Has it happened yet, or is that still in store for us? We stole its tongue. Or we *will* steal its tongue. Ripped from its mouth by the hunter of tongues. Can its owner sense it digesting inside my stomach? Has the tongue drawn it back to claim what belongs to it? Except, what we heard outside was clearly a man, a man with a tongue. But what had he been shooting? Something with a strong sense of smell. Something that likes to suck on fingers . . .

. . . Unless I'm not the hunter of tongues yet, then maybe . . . maybe tonight this guy with the machine gun returns . . . sniffing out our fingers . . . pretending to be Spot . . . claiming to be a good boy . . .

No. That already happened.

This is something new.

Oh *god* what is *happening* out there?

I can't hold it in any longer. "Do you think . . . do you think maybe this is . . . you know . . . the devil . . . ?"

"If it is," Dad says, "he sure as fuck knows how to make an entrance."

"Mom? What do you think?"

"I don't know what I believe," she says.

"Because you're an atheist?"

"I'm too tired and hungry to think clearly about anything."

"Are we going to die here?" I ask.

"I don't know."

"Oh, god."

Dad stares into the crack again. "Imagine the fucking irony of escaping, only to get mowed down by some maniac with a gun . . . shit, what the fuck is going on out there?"

"If it is," I say, "uh . . . demons . . . and hell . . . do you think . . . uh . . . do you think someone could have . . . you know . . . "

He turns toward me. "Could have what?"

" . . . Caused it?"

"*Caused* it?"

"Yeah. Like. One person. If they could have the ability to make . . . uh . . . I don't know, the ground open up or whatever."

"I don't know what you're talking about."

"Like witchcraft or something."

"I don't know how this works, Mel."

"I just wondered if maybe they made it happen, if they could also make it stop. Like . . . if they could fix things."

Dad sighs and rests his head against the wall, breathing heavy, not saying anything until he takes a deep whiff and grimaces. "Ugh. We reek."

We take turns using the shower. When one of us hops in, the other three face the opposite direction, giving our best attempt at providing some semblance of privacy. Bobby goes first and lets out a shriek as the cold water sprays him directly in the face and I can't prevent the laughter from spilling out.

"Don't laugh, Sis! It's not funny."

"It's a little funny," I call out over my shoulder.

"Your big stupid butt is funny, Sis!"

"Shut up, Bobby. No it's not."

"Yes it is!" He howls with laughter as the water pours down him. "It's funny because it's full of farts!"

"Oh my god. Gross."

"Your butt is full of a million farts, Sis! And they all smell like . . . like farts! Like old, disgusting, smelly, rotten . . . *farts!*"

We use the same towel to dry off, then change back into our dirty clothes and apply an abundant amount of deodorant. We spend an extraordinary amount of time brushing our teeth. Somehow we end up tricking ourselves that we feel reinvigorated.

"We should have done this a while ago," Mom says.

"Yeah," Bobby says, "because Sissy's butt was starting to smell, right?"

"Shut up," I tell him.

"We were all stinky," Mom says.

"Even you?" Bobby asks.

She nods, serious. "Even me."

He frowns and rubs his stomach. "I'm so hungry."

"I know, baby."

"When are we going to eat?"

"I don't know."

"I want an omelet. I want an omelet with ham and extra cheese."

"How much cheese?"

"All of the cheese in the world."

"That's it?"

"Yeah, only that much. But Sissy doesn't get any

cheese. Only I get the cheese. Right?" He taps my shoulder. "You hear that, Sis? You don't get any of the cheese. Only I—"

But I'm no longer listening to him.

Ahead, on the floor, slithering inside the bathroom through the cracked-open door . . .

A snake.

Not just any normal gardening snake, either, but a big . . . thick . . . fucking . . . snake.

Brown, with a dark diamond pattern spiraling down the back of its scales.

I extend out my arm, pointing at it.

"What . . . what . . . what . . . what . . . "

Slowly, the rest of them follow my gaze.

It finishes entering the bathroom before any of us have time to process what we're experiencing.

Bobby and I scream and backpedal against the wall, holding on to each other. Mom joins us seconds later. Dad, on the other hand, remains perfectly still next to the door, eyes bulging as he witnesses the rattlesnake approaching his feet. He looks at the snake, then us, then the snake.

"What . . . what do I do?" he whispers.

"Don't move," Mom says. "Maybe it'll go away."

The rattlesnake slithers over Dad's shoe, perfectly at peace with the universe.

"Get this fucking thing away from me," Dad says.

"It'll only bite you if it feels threatened," Mom tells him.

"Fuck that. Come help me."

"Stop talking. Calm down."

"Fuck you. *You* calm down. You're not the one with a fucking rattlesnake dry-humping your leg."

Bobby laughs through his tears.

"Be quiet," Mom says.

"But Daddy said humping," Bobby says, wiping snot from his face.

"Goddammit," Dad says, "this isn't fucking funny. It's gonna fucking bite me. I just know it. Goddammit. Shit. Shit. Fucking *shit*. Fuck. Fuck. *Fuuuuuck*."

The rattlesnake slithers off his foot and the moment it's no longer engaging in any physical contact, my father tries to edge away. His movement provokes the snake's rattler. Dad screams and leaps onto the sink just as the snake strikes out at his leg, barely missing him. Most of the supplies Mom had rested on the counter scatter to the floor, further startling the snake.

Everybody's screaming now.

Dad's completely on top of the sink, looking down at the rattlesnake and flipping it two middle fingers.

"Yeah! Fuck you, snake! I'll fucking eat your family for breakfast, you motherfucker!"

The snake does not seem fazed by these insults.

The rest of us pile into the tub, embracing each other, shaking, nobody taking our eyes off the snake that's now slithering to the center of the bathroom, on my dead grandma's repulsive blanket. Its rattler won't quit going off, like a phone's weather alert screaming about impending doom. It stops between the tub and toilet and settles into a ball.

"Did it bite you?" Mom asks Dad.

"I don't know. I don't think so." Standing on the toilet, he inspects his legs, then shrugs. "I don't feel anything." It's a miracle he doesn't lose his balance, hunched over like that.

"That was close," Mom says.

"Yeah, no shit."

"Where did it come from?" I ask.

"Someone has to put it in a basket," Bobby says.

"*What?*"

"That's where rattlesnakes go. In baskets. I saw a guy do it on YouTube."

Dad lowers his jaw, at a loss for words. "Nobody's putting that fucking thing in a basket, you lunatic."

"What are we going to do then?" Bobby asks.

"Maybe it'll just . . . just get bored and go back out the way it came," Mom says.

"But what if it doesn't?"

" . . . I guess we'll cross that road when we get to it."

Dad suddenly starts laughing. "One fucking thing after another. Jesus *Christ*. Can't we get one fucking break?"

Outside, thunder cracks and heavy rain begins to fall, and we're all gasping and holding each other tighter, except for my father.

His laughter only seems to get louder.

"I ever tell you guys I used to have a snake as a pet, back when I was a kid?" Dad says, still hiding on top of the sink. The snake hasn't left the middle of the bathroom. It's made itself at home here with us. No way is it going anywhere any time soon.

Bobby's the only one who acts like he's interested in what our father has to say. "You *did?*"

Dad nods. "Mmm-hm. Sure did. A python."

Bobby points at the snake on the floor. "Is that a python?"

"I don't think it is."

"Then what is it, Daddy?"

Dad takes his time answering, inspecting the creature a little longer, as if he's suddenly some snake expert now, which of course he isn't. "You know, Bobby, I'm not exactly sure."

"It's obviously a rattlesnake," I tell them.

"Why do you say that?" Dad says.

"Because it has a rattler."

Dad's quiet for a moment. "That doesn't mean anything. Lots of snakes have rattlers. Not just rattlesnakes."

I want to call him a liar. I want to accuse him of not knowing what the hell he's talking about. I want to tell him he's so full of shit it's overflowing from his eyeballs. What's he gonna do? Get off the counter and try knocking some sense into me? Fat chance. Not with a snake between us. I open my mouth to let loose on him, but Mom pinches my arm and gives me a *please don't* look, so I fall quiet.

Dad waits a moment to make sure I'm done, then continues. "You wanna know what his name was? My snake?"

"What?" Bobby asks, eager to find out.

"Monty."

"What?"

"*Monty.*"

"Oh." Bobby frowns. "Why?"

"Because of . . . you know . . . he was a python."

"Oh. Okay."

"What's the matter with you? You don't know Monty Python now?"

"Robert, why would he know what Monty Python is?" Mom asks.

"What's Monty Python?" I ask, feeling dumb for having to ask the question.

Dad sighs. "Jesus Christ. You two. How are you even mine?"

"Sometimes I wonder the same thing," I reply, not realizing what I actually said until the words left my mouth.

But instead of screaming, he only lets out a soft laugh. "At least we know you're your mother's."

"What's that supposed to mean?" Mom says.

"I think he's calling me a bitch," I tell her, enjoying the word as it leaves my mouth. *Bitch bitch bitch.* I can almost taste it.

Dad grins and he's never looked more like a villain.

"What happened to the snake?" Bobby asks. "What happened to Monkey?"

"*Monty,*" Dad says. "His name was *Monty.*"

"What happened to Monty?"

"Well, I'll tell you what happened," Dad says, licking his lips. "I loved that snake. I loved it so much. It was my favorite thing in the world. My mom, she got it for me for my birthday when I turned nine. I don't even know why. I don't think I had asked for one. I guess she just thought it would be a good gift. Or maybe she got a good deal. My mom, your grandmother, she's always been talented at getting good deals. What I remember most about the snake is how I'd take him out of his cage, or whatever it's called, the terrarium? I'd take him out and let him wrap around my neck and I'd walk around the house with Monty like he was a scarf."

"Dad! You can't do that!"

"Why not?"

"Snakes will bite you."

Dad shakes his head. "No, Monty was a good snake. He wasn't a violent one or anything. He didn't have any poison in him."

"*Venom*," Bobby says. "He didn't have any *venom* in him."

"Whatever the fuck. Who cares? The point is. He was my snake. And then one day, I come home from school and guess what? The terrarium's empty. The lid's been knocked off somehow and Monty's nowhere in sight."

"He escaped?"

Dad nods. "He escaped."

"Where did he go?"

"We weren't sure at first. I searched up and down the house the rest of the day, tearing everything apart trying to find him, but he was nowhere in sight. Almost like he'd never existed at all, you know? Like we made him up."

"Like an imaginary friend?" Bobby says.

"Yeah, just like an imaginary friend, but that couldn't be, right? I mean, we had the terrarium and everything. He'd been real. But where did he go?"

"Maybe someone broke in and stole him?"

Dad doesn't respond at first. His focus seems to drift off to the corner of the room. Then he snaps back awake. "You know, that's funny."

"What?"

WE NEED TO DO SOMETHING

"Of all the possibilities that ran through my head back then, when I was a kid, I don't think that ever even occurred to me, that some . . . some *house burglar* might've been responsible. Some guy, some weirdo pervert going around sneaking into all the houses in my neighborhood, stealing everybody's pets."

"I hope he didn't put them all in the same bag," Bobby says. "Not all pets get along. Sometimes they fight."

"That's very true. Sometimes pets fight."

"Well what *happened?*"

"We started hearing noises in the walls. Like, loud thuds. Crawling."

Bobby goes wide-eyed. "The snake got into *the wall?*"

"Exactly."

"But *how?*"

"My old house growing up, we used to have a real bad issue with mice. I remember sometimes waking up in the middle of the night, sitting up in bed, and seeing them on my bedroom floor. Just . . . I don't know what they were doing. I used to think they were watching me sleep."

"Do mice watch people sleep?" Bobby asks, concerned.

"These mice did."

"I don't think I like mice."

"Nobody does, son." He massages his temple, wincing. "But not long after Monty disappeared into the walls, something happened."

"What?"

"The mice also disappeared."

"Where'd they go?"

"Monty started eating them all. I think he got into the wall by slithering into a mouse hole, then just slaughtered every last one of those fuckers. Ate them up one by one. Total goddamn buffet."

"Wow. He must've gotten so fat."

"The fattest snake in Texas."

Bobby points at the rattlesnake on the bathroom floor. "This one's fat, too."

Dad nods. "He's a big boy."

"What do you think is in his belly?"

"I don't know, Bobby."

We sit and watch the snake lounge for a while. What else can we do? The thing has us hostage.

"Wait," Bobby says later on. "What ever happened to Monty, Daddy?"

"What?"

"Did you ever see him again, after he went into the walls and ate all the mice?"

Dad nods, a sudden sadness washed over him. "Only one more time." He hesitates, refusing to look at us. "One night, almost a year after he escaped, I woke up in bed to something tight around my throat. It was him. It was Monty. He'd come back to me."

"What?" Bobby says, excited. "Wow!"

"Yeah." Dad sighs. "Slithered up into my bed and wrapped himself around my neck. Scared the shit out of me. I started screaming and freaking out. My mom, your grandmother, she comes running in and flips on the light, sees me in bed with my snake around my neck and screams just as loud as I did."

"Then what happened?"

"Well. I unwrapped Monty from my neck and discovered he was dead. That's what happened."

"*Dead?* How?"

Dad shrugs. "I don't know. I guess it was just his time."

Bobby pouts. "That's a sad story, Dad!"

"I know. I'm sorry." He closes his eyes and leans against the mirror. "You know, I've thought about that night a lot, and there's something I've never been able to figure out."

"Figure out what?" Bobby asks.

"Whether or not he came back because he wanted to be with someone he loved as he died, or . . . "

"Or what?"

He leans forward, eyes open, expression blank. " . . . or if he was trying to take me with him."

"I used to be dead," Amy's telling me. It's the day after Joe died. The bathroom's gone. The snake's gone. My family's gone. My body melts down the drain and transports me to Amy's house. Empty again. We ditched the rest of the day following our homeroom teacher's announcement, went back to her place. Her parents will be at work until five or six. Until then, we have the house to ourselves. Under other circumstances we might be taking advantage of this alone time with more pleasure. Today, however, we hold each other on the couch in the living room, trying not to cry and failing. Well, at least I'm failing. Amy seems bizarrely calm about the whole thing.

"I know," I tell her. "You told me."

"But haven't you ever wondered what changed? What fixed me?"

"Sure." She's ignoring the fact that I've asked her before, numerous times actually, and she's always dodged the question.

"It was a spell," she says now.

"Like what we did to Joe?"

" . . . Not exactly."

"What do you mean, not exactly?"

"We're talking, like, super black magic shit."

"The tongue spell wasn't black magic?"

"More like black magic for beginners. Amateurs."

I sit up from her embrace and face her on the couch. "Amy. He *died*. We *killed* him."

"I know. We fucked up."

"We?"

She nods. "We're in this together, aren't we?"

I hesitate, thinking it wasn't *my* idea to seek hoodoo vengeance, but it wasn't like I'd tried to stop her, either. I'd been fully on board until the real consequences sunk in. Claiming anything else would only be hypocritical and false. "Yes." Our fingertips connect. "We're in this together."

She smiles faintly. "Thank you for not abandoning me."

"I would never."

She leans over and kisses me. I kiss her back. Then she parts from my mouth and whispers, "It was a necromancy spell."

"A *what*?"

"Necromancy."

"Like, raising the dead?"

Amy nods. "I found one buried on the occult subreddit. No one really took it seriously. It only had a couple comments. Something that was posted and ignored. But I found it."

"That's what we used on Joe?"

"No, Melli, not Joe. *Me*. I used it on myself."

"You used a necromancy spell on yourself?"

"I told you. I was dead. Or, at least, I thought I was dead. That's up for speculation, I guess."

"H-h-how? What happened?"

She shrugs. "It was complicated, and getting into the details now . . . it's not important, right? The point is this: necromancy was supposed to bring back the dead, and something inside me was dead, so it only made sense—theoretically, at least—that it could— *would*—work."

"And it did?"

"I think so?"

"What do you mean?"

"I thought I was better, that I was healed."

"And you're not?"

"I haven't felt right for the past couple days. I thought maybe it was just all the deepfake bullshit. But now I suspect it's something else. Something a little more evil."

"Amy, you're not making any sense."

"What if it wasn't me who was really dead all this time? What if something *else* was inside me, and that's what was dead? And when I performed the necromancy spell . . . it woke up? And it's just been . . . I don't know, biding its time, waiting for the perfect moment to announce its arrival?"

"Something like *what*?"

"I don't know. A demon, I guess. Something from another realm. A malevolent spirit of some kind. I think maybe it's been attached to me all my life, and I fucked up, gave it permission to stretch its legs."

I reach forward and caress her cheek. "You're not evil. I would know."

"Think about the deepfake video Joe made."

"What about it?"

"Just, like, the concept, you know? Replacing one face over another. Masks over masks. What if I'm the deepfake, and the demon inside me is the real deal? The real *me*."

"Amy, I—"

"It has to be why the tongue spell went so wrong. I know, we substituted a dog's tongue for a cow's, but still, I mean *holy shit*, there's no way what happened should have happened. Unless, the person who conducted the ritual had something hiding inside them, something beyond human. Something . . . "

"Something what?"

" . . . something diabolical."

I snap awake to the sound of Bobby whining about having to pee. I glance around, searching for Amy, but she's long gone. Was she ever really here? Goddammit, I'm losing my mind. Bobby keeps whining until Mom and Dad wake up. Dad had passed out in the sink basin, the faucet driving into his spine, which he complains about the moment he regains consciousness. His arms knock over various bottles of gels and soaps as he struggles to free himself from the dip.

We scan the bathroom floor. No sign of the snake.

"Do you think it went back outside?" I ask.

"I don't see it anywhere," Dad says.

"I think it left," Bobby says. "It got mad it couldn't eat any of us so it went back home to pout."

"Who saw it last?" Mom asks.

"I fell asleep," I whisper.

"We all fell asleep," Dad says.

We spend the next minute staring at the empty floor.

"Shit," Mom says.

"What?" I ask.

"Where did it go?"

"Like you said before. Maybe it went out the way it came."

"Yeah. Maybe."

Bobby holds his crotch, body trembling between us. "I gotta pee I gotta pee I gotta pee."

"Pee in the tub," Mom tells him. "It's not safe."

"Gross!" I cry out. "No! Do *not* pee in the tub."

"I'm gonna pee all over you, Sis!"

"Mom! Don't let him pee in the tub! Please . . ."

She sighs. "Okay. Hold on. Just . . . just hold on."

She leans over the tub, peering around the bathroom. No snake in sight. "Do you see anything?" she asks Dad.

He hesitates, curses under his breath, then plops down to the floor. He crouches and walks around, scanning the room. Finally, he straightens back up and shakes his head. "It must have left while we were asleep."

"Can I *please* pee now?"

Dad approaches the tub and helps Bobby out, who rushes over to the toilet and releases a long pleasurable moan as the urine splashes against the water. "I love peeing," he sings, "I love peeing, ooooh I love to pee all day and all night . . . "

"Will you shut up?" I say, still in the tub. No way in hell am I ever getting out of this thing again.

"Watch me shake my booty, Sis! Watch me shake my booty!"

He indeed shakes his booty at me as he pees, no doubt spraying urine all over the floor next to the toilet. Eventually, thank god, the stream comes to an end, and he reaches down to flush.

Then he shrieks and tries to step away from the toilet, only to fall flat on his back.

Holding his wrist against his chest.

Body shaking.

Sobbing hysterically.

The rattlesnake slithers out from behind the toilet.

"*Fuck fuck fuck fuck fuck,*" someone's screaming, and I realize it's all three of us, together, as a family.

Dad grabs Bobby by the shirt collar and drags him across the bathroom. Mom tries to help with his feet, but gets too close to the snake. It's rising as if to attack again. She steps away, never taking her eyes off the thing. I stay in the bathtub. Sucking on my thumb like I've reverted to infancy. Rocking back and forth. Pathetic. Worthless. When the shit hits the fan, this is all the help I can provide.

Mom crouches, maintaining eye contact with the snake, looking like they're in a surreal Old West flick and they're about to draw down on each other. Dad watches those kinds of movies all the time when he's drunk, which is always. Behind her, Bobby's shrieking off the top of his lungs. Dad's trying to inspect his wrist but Bobby won't let go of it with his other hand.

The snake looks *pissed* and ready to kill anyone who crosses its path.

This isn't happening this isn't happening this isn't happening.

Mom edges to the side, next to the sink, and in one quick motion picks up the trash can, flips it upside down, and brings it over the snake just as it strikes out at her, successfully trapping it inside. Random garbage spills out along the floor, including the empty bottle of mouthwash. For extra effect, she grabs the toilet tank lid and rests it on top of the can, weighing it down against the floor.

She turns away and hurries to Bobby. Dad's hovering over him, paralyzed with fear. She brushes him away and takes control of the situation, snapping her fingers in front of Bobby's eyes until he stops screaming and pays attention, confused and afraid but no longer hysterical.

"It got you?" she asks.

Bobby nods, frantic. "Uh-huh."

"Let me see."

"It *huuuurrrts.*"

"Let me see, baby."

Hesitating, he uncurls his uninjured hand and reveals the bite mark on his left wrist. Even from the bathtub I can spot the two puncture wounds. Thin lines of blood trickle out of them. Mom points at Dad and tells him to give her his belt.

"What? Why?"

"We need to make a tourniquet."

Dad shakes his head. "No. We need to suck the poison out."

"What?"

"That's what they always do in movies. They suck the poison out."

" . . . I think we need to prevent the poison from flowing to his heart. Take your belt off."

"Venom!" Bobby shouts through his sobbing, and they both look down at him, confused. "Snakes have venom, not poison!"

Dad sighs and removes his belt, then hands it over to her. She wraps it around Bobby's forearm and tightens it into place. The whole time Bobby's screaming his head off and she's trying to shush him as motherly as possible. My focus pinballs from my brother to the upside-down trash can across the bathroom. It keeps shaking, and inside the snake's rattler hasn't shut up. It doesn't want us to forget it's still here, ready to inject its venom into the rest of us the moment we give it a chance.

Dad kneels and grabs Bobby's injured arm and pulls it toward his mouth. "We gotta suck the poison out—the *venom*. Otherwise he's gonna die."

When Dad says this, Bobby lets loose with another shriek. Mom stares at Dad, paralyzed with indecision, but he doesn't wait for her approval. He brings the bite wound to his mouth and sucks down for several seconds, then grimaces and pulls away, gagging and spitting.

"Did you get it?" Mom asks. "Did you get it?"

"I don't know." Dad wipes his mouth, disgusted. "Maybe."

He starts gagging again, prompting him to hurry to the sink and lower his face under the faucet. It doesn't take long for him to choke on the water pouring down his throat. He gives up and rests his forehead against the wall, out of breath, wheezing.

Meanwhile, Bobby's still groaning and writhing on the floor. Mom helps him to his feet and together they get into the tub with me. I try to scoot to the side and give them plenty of room, but two seconds of the faucet digging into my spine is all the motivation I need to relinquish my porcelain grave. Mom scoops up the blanket from the floor and spreads it along the tub, then helps Bobby sprawl across it.

"You'll be safer here, baby."

"It hurts. It *huuurrrts.*"

"I know, baby. It's going to be okay, it's going to be okay."

"Did Daddy get the venom out?"

"Yes. He got it all out. You're going to be just fine."

Dad starts pacing around the bathroom, fists at his side, jaw clenched, rambling. "That motherfucker . . . that fucking . . . that fucking motherfucker . . . " He points at the upside-down trash can with intense rage. "*You motherfucking motherfucker!*"

I fold my arms across my chest, barely dodging my father's erratic movements. "Is Bobby going to be okay? Mom, is Bobby going to be okay?"

"He's going to be just fine." Mom smiles at a terrified Bobby. "Isn't that right, baby? You're going to be just fine, right?"

"Y-y-y-yes?"

Mom searches frantically through the various bathroom items scattered across the floor and counter until finding the tall bottle of peroxide. She unscrews the lid, tells Bobby it's going to hurt, and splashes some of it along his arm without waiting for a response.

Bobby clutches the wound and wails.

Off in the corner, I'm hugging myself and trying not to cry, whispering, "This is all my fault this is all my fault this is all my fault—"

"Am I going to need to see a doctor?" Bobby asks.

"Sure, just to be safe," Mom says. "Once we get out of here."

"But what if that man shoots us?"

" . . . We don't know what that was."

"*These motherfuckers!*" Dad screams, and charges the bathroom door. I leap out of the way just as he connects with the wood and bounces back on the floor. No visible damage is inflicted.

He remains flat on his back, staring up at the ceiling, breathing heavily, seething.

I step into the tub with Bobby and Mom and the three of us watch him, waiting to see what's going to happen next.

In a voice so low and calm we can barely hear him, Dad says, "Why hasn't he come to check on you yet?"

Another long silence.

And I can't take it any longer. "Why hasn't *who—*"

"Dee," Dad says, cutting me off, "don't play deaf. I know you heard me." He sits up and glares at her.

"It's been a week. Maybe longer. Don't you think he's worried about you?"

"I don't want to do this right now," Mom tells him. "Not in front of the kids."

Dad rubs his brow, annoyed. "I'm not trying to be an asshole, goddammit. I'm just saying. We need to get out of here or we're all fucked. Especially now with Bobby. Is there a chance he might come?"

"Who are you guys talking about?" I ask, practically pleading at this point.

Mom doesn't answer.

"Well?" Dad says, voice prodding.

She sighs. "I told him if he didn't hear from me by midnight, that something might have happened."

Dad narrows his eyes. "Something like what?"

"We shouldn't get into this right now."

He makes a big show of looking around the bathroom. "Oh, do you have a better time in mind? Maybe go out in the living room and continue this discussion, is that it?"

"You can't go to the living room," Bobby says, voice weak. "We're stuck."

"Thank you, Bobby. I guess I forgot."

"You're welcome."

"What's going on?" I ask again.

Dad cocks his head at Mom. "Dee?"

"I didn't know how you'd react. I was scared."

"Scared of what?"

" . . . of you."

Dad laughs. "What did you think I'd do? *Hurt* you?"

"Maybe."

"Jesus fucking Christ." He wipes his lips. "Have I

ever hurt you?" He gestures to me and Bobby. "Have I ever hurt your mom? Huh?"

"Sometimes you yell and get angry and make her cry," Bobby tells him.

This response seems to sucker punch Dad into silence.

A half hour passes. Or maybe an entire day. Eventually Mom says, "If he was going to come, he would have already been here."

"Where does he live?"

"Not far. Within walking distance."

"Jesus fuck."

I can feel the rage boiling inside me, much how I imagine it permanently cooks in my father. "*Stop ignoring me!*"

Everybody directs their attention my way. Like they just realized I've been trapped in this bathroom with them the entire time. I can't stop shaking.

"What are you *talking* about?" I ask them.

Of course I'm met by another long silence.

"*Hello?*"

Dad lowers his head, quiet.

Mom clears her throat. "Your father and I are getting a divorce."

"*What?*"

"No you're not!" Bobby shouts from the tub. "That's not true. Dad, tell Mom to stop lying."

Dad remains unresponsive.

"We decided on it the night of the tornado," Mom says. "We were going to tell you both the next day."

Dad snorts. "*We* decided?"

Realization hits. All the clues, right in my face this

entire time. "Oh my god, Mom, are you cheating on Dad?"

"I've been seeing someone. Yes. He makes me happy. I deserve to be happy."

"And I don't?" Dad asks.

"Goddammit, Robert, don't pull that shit now."

"Pull *what* shit?"

"I tried. I fucking *tried*. And I was miserable. I asked you to get sober. I asked you to help out more. I fucking *begged you*, Robert. I *begged you*."

"I can't believe you guys are getting a divorce," I whisper.

"Who are we going to live with?" Bobby whines.

And I tell him, "Mom, obviously."

Dad glares at me, hurt. "Why obviously?"

He catches me off guard. I realize I've screwed up. "I don't know."

"No. You said obviously. What the fuck did you mean by obviously?"

"Just . . . you know . . . I don't . . . I don't . . . "

Mom takes over for me. "She meant that I'm the only one who can actually take care of them without passing out drunk in the front yard."

"That was one time."

"It shouldn't have been *any* times."

"Guys . . . " Bobby whispers.

But Dad ignores him and stands back up, getting that crazy look in his eyes again. "You think you're taking my children away from me, you got another thing coming, baby. You fuckin' try it. I dare you."

"...*guys*..."

"Please stop fighting," I chant, "please stop fighting please stop fighting please—"

Mom takes in the whole situation and does something peculiar. She smirks. "You're scaring the kids again, dear."

Dad stops and glares at us all in the tub, seething with rage, then reality hits and he points at Bobby. "What's wrong with him?"

We all glance down and discover Bobby convulsing in the tub next to us. He's grabbing his wrist and moaning. We rush on top of him, trying to calm him down.

"*It hurts,*" he cries, "*it hurts it hurts it's on FIRE I'm on FIRE help me HELP ME . . .*"

"The belt's making it worse," Dad says. "You're fucking killing him."

"*. . . oh my GOD oh my GOD . . .*"

Frantic, Mom loosens the belt and casts it aside, nearly slapping me in the face with it in the process. Bobby continues moaning. His wrist and hand have gotten extremely swollen and discolored. She hesitates, examining it, clearly out of her element just like the rest of us. She twists the tub faucet to COLD.

"Put it under the water, baby. Come on."

Bobby scoots up to the flowing water and cautiously extends his arm under the faucet. He cries out and hides his hand against his chest. "*IT HURTS IT HURTS EVERYTHING BURNS!*"

Mom presses her own hand against his chest, waiting, concentrating, then withdraws. "Oh, god, his heartbeat is way too fast."

Dad kneels so they're eye-level. "Bobby, calm the fuck down! You gotta calm the fuck down right now!"

This only makes Bobby cry louder and further freak out.

"That isn't helping," Mom says.

"Well what the fuck do you want me to do, then?"

"I don't know."

"We have to do *something*, don't we?" I wail. "We have to do *something*."

Mom soothes her voice down into something replicating calmness. "Okay, baby, take big deep breaths, okay? Real nice and easy now. It's going to be okay. It's going to be okay . . ."

They continue this routine for several minutes and eventually he actually starts to calm down. Mom cradles him in her arms. They're both dripping with sweat and tears and—judging by the smell—urine.

"Can you tell me, Momma?" Bobby asks, voice soft.

"Tell you what, baby?"

"You know."

Dad's sitting on the toilet, next to the upside-down trash can. The snake has stopped moving for the time being. Its rattler no longer makes any noise. Perhaps it's trying to fool us into believing it's gone away and that we're safe. Stupid snake. There's no way in hell any of us are ever going to entertain such a fantastical delusion again.

Mom holds Bobby tighter, resting her cheek against the back of his head. "Well, we were at Walmart trying to buy a frozen pizza, and you decided you had been in my belly long enough."

"Your big fat belly," Bobby whispers, a faint trace of humor lingering in his tone.

Mom nods. "Like a watermelon."

Bobby lets out a soft laugh.

"And I couldn't walk any more, it hurt so bad, you

were kicking me so much, so I had to sit on the floor right there in the frozen food aisle, and Sissy had to go find someone to help us."

"Did they call an ambulance?"

"They sure did. So we waited for it to arrive and this very nice, young cashier sat with me holding my hand telling me everything was going to be okay, that I just had to be strong and wait a little bit longer and nothing bad would happen and everything would work out, just like now, baby, just how I'm holding you and telling you the same thing because it's the truth, baby, you know that, right? It's going to be okay, it's going to be okay, it's going to be okay, it's going to be okay."

A fresh wave of tears stream down Mom's face as she chokes back sobs and continues.

"And I asked the cashier, the young lady, I asked her how she could know it was going to be okay, and she looked down at me and smiled this wonderful bright smile and do you know what she told me, baby? She told me she knew it was all going to be okay because it *had* to be. You get it? It was going to be okay because it couldn't possibly be any other way. That we just had to believe it would be okay and act brave and strong and it would all work out, and you know what, baby? She was right. She helped me act brave and strong and we waited for the ambulance to arrive and they pulled you out of me right there in the frozen food aisle and I saw your beautiful little face in the paramedic's arms and I knew in that moment that I should have never doubted my love for you and that I would never ever doubt it again and I *haven't,* I never have, and that's why I know you're going to be okay and Sissy's going to be okay and everything's going to be okay so we just have to hang on a little bit longer and someone will come, I know it, someone will come and they'll move the tree and open the door and everybody will be waiting outside to make sure we're okay and life will be better, I promise you, sweet beautiful baby, I promise with every ounce of my soul everything is going to be okay, you just have to trust me, okay, baby? You have to trust."

She cries and rocks Bobby in her arms and his eyes are half-open but he's no longer breathing, and we all know it, we've known it for several minutes now, but that doesn't stop her from rocking him, from holding him tighter and spitting tears and mucus from her mouth as all of the world's agony blossoms into its final form.

"Fuck this," Dad says, and rips open the box of alcohol wipes and shoves several in his mouth. He chews them like gum, sucking up their juices and spitting them out once they're dry. His face twists with agony but still he throws another handful of wipes in his mouth. Pacing the bathroom. Chewing. Sucking. Spitting. I don't know if those will actually get him drunk and I doubt he knows, either. But goddammit, he's going to try.

Bobby hasn't left the tub. The blanket's wrapped around his body, hiding his flesh from view. Mom sits on the floor just outside the tub, back leaning against the porcelain, jaw against chest, eyes closed. Once I thought this tub would serve as my own grave. How foolish I had been. Perhaps soon enough, we will all follow my brother into the unknown.

I keep waiting for him to jump up and shout, *Gotcha!* Anything to confirm he's pulling some kind of prank. It wouldn't be the first time he's pretended to be dead or kidnapped for a laugh. I remember once he said something particularly asshole-ish to me, so I punched him in the stomach and he doubled over and collapsed to the floor. Rolled his eyes back and lolled his tongue out and everything. Got completely still, wouldn't move or acknowledge our demands for him to knock it off. Finally, after Mom started to really freak out, he sat up and apologized, said he was just trying to scare us.

Well, if that's all he's doing now, he's definitely succeeding.

We're scared, all right.

We're fucking terrified.

How can a kid go from making butt jokes one second, then . . . then . . . then . . .

Oh my god. How can this be real?

I stand in the center of the bathroom, unsure which parent to focus on. None of us can stop crying. I need them both to hear what I have to say but I don't want to tell it to either of them. How am I supposed to explain something I barely understand? How sure am I my memories are even real? How long have we been in this fucking bathroom? It's impossible to separate facts from fictions. Maybe Amy never existed. Maybe the black magic rituals were invented inside a brain rotting with slow, impending death.

No.

It happened.

I know it was real. Otherwise, nothing else is real, either. This bathroom. My family. These thoughts. I might as well be throwing a temper tantrum in some mental asylum, confined by a straitjacket drenched in my own slobber.

"This is all my fault," I finally whisper to the room.

Slowly, both my parents lift their heads. Eyes black from sleep deprivation. Skin loose around their faces. They just stare at me for a moment, as if they're not sure I spoke.

"What?" Mom says.

"I said this is all my fault."

"What's all your fault, honey?"

I pause, unsure how to answer such a complex question, then point at the bathroom door, followed by the bathtub.

"What are you talking about?" she says.

"This all happened because of me."

"No it didn't, honey. C'mon. Don't think like that. It's nobody's fault."

"No. Listen. You aren't listening. You never listen."

"Okay."

"Last night." I shake my head. "No. Not last night. Not anymore. The night it started. When was that? That night . . . that night . . . Amy and I . . . we did something bad. We did something real bad."

No one responds. I have their attention now.

"There's a website we go to sometimes."

"What kind of website?" Dad asks. He's still chewing those alcohol wipes. The sound's sickening and I can't stand to hear it.

"Please don't get mad," I tell them.

"Mel, what the hell are you talking about?"

"It was like a subreddit thing. Like, for the occult. People all around sharing . . . I don't know, books they've found."

"Books?"

"Like, old books. PDFs, blogs, Google docs. Everything."

"What are you talking about?"

"I'm saying, this subreddit, what they had. I guess . . . spells, basically. Like, I don't know, rituals."

"What the fuck is a *subreddit*?" Dad asks, but I ignore him. Despite our current predicament of being trapped in a bathroom, there is still not enough time to thoroughly explain Reddit to my father in a way that he will comprehend.

"I don't understand, honey," Mom says.

"Amy was sick, okay? Like . . . really, truly sick."

"What do you mean? What was wrong with her? Was it cancer? Did she have cancer?"

Shit, how the hell am I supposed to explain this? Especially after everything that's happened. It'll sound like I'm speaking in a foreign language (*speaking in tongues*). I inhale and exhale deep breaths several times before continuing. "We thought, maybe, there was something inside her. Something . . . bad, like . . . like a spirit. Or . . . or a demon." I hate how silly it sounds coming out of my mouth. It makes me feel like a little kid.

126

Dad lets out a loud laugh. "Mel, what the fuck are you babbling about?"

"It was ruining her life." I try sounding more serious by deepening my voice and waving my hands to punctuate certain words. "The thing inside her. It used to be dead, but then it came to life, and it wanted to destroy her, wanted to take over her body and do bad things."

"Just be quiet, okay?" Dad says. "You're delirious. Close your eyes. Go back to sleep."

"Bad things like what?" Mom asks, voice cracking.

"Like . . . like . . . you remember that boy from my school, the one who died?"

"What?" Dad says.

Mom nods. "They sent an email out about it."

"What email?" Dad says. "I didn't get no fuckin' email."

"They probably don't have yours listed."

"And why the hell not?"

"Probably because you never gave it to them."

"Well, why didn't you?"

"Why didn't I *what*, Robert?"

"Give them my fuckin' email."

"Because I already gave them mine."

"Will you guys please stop fighting?" I ask them, nearly yelling. "Jesus *Christ*. Please. Just . . . just let me say what I have to say." What I don't point out is they're arguing about a goddamn email address less than five feet from their dead son. His body rapidly decomposing and still they have to bicker about things that don't matter. What I don't tell them is they should have never gotten married, that they could have easily spared us all future horrors by simply dissolving their relationship long before having children. Our existence has been a burden on not only them but also ourselves since day one in the womb.

"Okay," Mom says. "I'm sorry."

"The boy who died . . . it was because of us. Amy and I, we performed a spell, something to make him stop spreading rumors, to stop making up lies. He wasn't supposed to die. That was never part of the plan. But . . . something went wrong. The spirit inside Amy, somehow it twisted the spell, made everything worse, and . . . and . . . and . . . he died. We did a tongue spell on him and that same night he choked on his tongue while sleeping."

"It's impossible to choke on your own tongue," Dad says, uncertain.

"Well, it happened. And who knows what would have kept happening if we didn't put an end to it?"

"What do you mean?" Mom says. "Put an end to—"

"—put an end to the thing possessing Amy."

"A demon," Dad says, no longer sounding so amused.

"We didn't know what it was, just that it was bad news."

"What did you do?"

I lick my lips and it takes me a moment to realize it's the same way Dad licks his own lips. I want to vomit but there's nothing left inside me to regurgitate besides hazy memories. "Amy found a PDF of this old grimoire, this—"

"An old *what*?" Dad says.

"Grimoire. Like . . . a textbook of magic. Old, super dark magic. It was called the *Black Pullet*."

"The *Black Bullet*?"

"*Pullet.*"

"Oh."

"It was really old," I tell them. "Like, from the seventeen-hundreds. Someone uploaded a PDF of it on the occult subreddit. I don't know how they had a copy, but they did. All those old books are on the internet, if you know where to search for them."

"And how did you know where to search for them?" he asks.

"I didn't. Amy did."

"Of course she did."

"What's that supposed to mean?" I ask, fists tightening at my sides. What am I going to do? Punch him? Shit, maybe.

He rolls his eyes. "Nothing."

I consider challenging him, but what's the point? This isn't about him. It never was. "We found this one spell in the book that looked promising. It said it had the power to destroy everything while also protecting your friends. We thought maybe we could direct it into the thing eating Amy from the inside. Channel all the magic into the evil force and destroy it once and for all. And, since it was also meant to protect friends, we thought Amy would be able to withstand it, that it would only harm the bad stuff inside her. At the time it was the only thing that made sense. We were so afraid something else would happen. We . . . we didn't know what else to do. Joe was dead and it was our fault and what if something like that happened again? We needed to get rid of the bad thing. We needed to kill it."

"So you did this ritual?" Mom asks.

I nod. "Yes."

"What happened?"

"We passed out at one point, inside the circle."

"What circle?"

"We made a circle out of salt. You know. For protection."

"Oh," Mom says.

Dad points at my arm. "Is that why you came home with a band-aid?"

I hold up my arm again, showing off the cut they'd long forgotten about until now. It's practically completely healed at this point, which worries me, because what does that mean for how much time has passed since the initial puncture? "The spell required a merging of blood."

"Jesus Christ." He laughs crazily. "You can't be fuckin' serious about any of this."

I nod at the bathtub, at what it holds. "Why would I lie?"

He stops laughing.

"When we woke up, nothing was different. We were both just . . . really tired. And it'd started raining. I asked Amy if it was gone and she didn't know. She had a headache and she felt sick to her stomach but she didn't know. It was raining so hard outside and I wanted to stay at her house but she said she needed to be alone, that I had to leave, and I couldn't stop crying because she'd never acted so distant before, so . . . so . . . so *mean*. She actually shoved me through the front door. Said I needed to go. Why would she do that? Why would she treat me like that after everything I did to help her?" I lick my lips again, just like my father, and continue before either of them have a chance to speak. "I ran home in the rain. Halfway here she texted me and apologized. She said she had to go to the bathroom and was embarrassed, that the spell must have affected her stomach funny. But I didn't believe her. It was obvious she was lying. I tried calling but she wouldn't answer the phone and it kept raining harder and harder and suddenly the tornado warnings kept popping up on my screen and I was freaking out, so I rushed the rest of the way home and you guys were all waiting for me in the living room, waiting to scream at me for not answering your dumb phone calls. Well now you guys know why I wasn't answering your fucking phone calls. I had much more important things going on. More important than any of you will ever understand. And I still don't know if she's okay. I don't know if she's alive or dead or what and there's nothing I can do to fix things because we're trapped in a goddamn fucking *bathroom* and now Bobby's dead and it's all my fault, the ritual did this, I know it did, it said it would destroy everything and that's exactly what it's doing. It's going to kill us all. Bobby was only the first to go."

Mom scoots closer, reaching out. "Oh, honey, that sounds like just a coincidence, you didn't—"

"You're right," Dad says, stone serious. We both turn toward him, caught off guard. "If that's true, what you said," he licks his lips, "why didn't you say anything before?"

"I-I-I was afraid."

"Brave enough to destroy the world, but too chickenshit to own up to it, huh?"

"What?"

"Robert—"

"—I want you to look in that tub. I want you to

look at your dead brother. Do you smell that? That's his body, decomposing. Rotting. And it's all because of you and your voodoo bitch girlfriend. I hope your fun little time on the internet was worth it. You've murdered your entire family because of it. The whole goddamn world, maybe."

I burst out crying and back up against the door, then slide down to my butt, holding my legs like, somehow, they'll protect me from his words. "I'm sorry I'm sorry I'm sorry I'm sorry I'm sorry . . . "

Mom stares at Dad, too shocked to say anything for a moment. "Speak like that to my daughter again and I'll slit your throat."

He grins. "I look forward to the day."

Something catches my eye on the floor next to the bottom of the sink counter. Almost hidden by shadows cast by the cabinet doors. I pick up the bottle and stare through tears at the NyQuil label. It's maybe three-fourths full. Amy would have had a field day with something like this.

Nighttime Relief the label promises, only I read it as *Nightmare Relief* instead, and that sounds pretty good right about now.

"What are you doing?" Mom asks.

"Sleeping," I whisper, unscrewing the white cap and raising it to my lips.

"Be careful with that," she tells me. "Only a little swig."

"Okay, Mom," I reply, and start chugging.

By the time she wrestles the bottle from my grasp there's nothing left inside it.

Five minutes later I can't keep my head up.

WE NEED TO DO SOMETHING

Mom's slapping me awake and I'm laughing because I can't feel her hand and I can't feel my cheek and I don't know why she's even bothering. I try telling her she'd have better luck slapping Bobby awake but I can't move my face, so how is it I'm laughing? Except it isn't my mother slapping me. It's Dad, and he's not slapping, he's punching, and his hand's drenched in my blood and it wasn't me laughing either, it was Dad the whole time, cackling and howling and screaming with laughter. I bite my tongue off and swallow it before he can steal it from me.

Someone's tickling my feet and my legs but when I look down there is nobody there and I try to scratch it but the sensation isn't external, it's deep inside my flesh and there's no escape, and I wish I wish I wish I didn't have legs and I wish I wish I wish I didn't have flesh and I wish I wish I wish I could invert my flesh inside out and rub my nerves against the floor like a dog satisfying a deep itch like a dog like a dog like a dog like Spot Spot Spot who's back Spot from the dead Spot from the grave Spot who is not a dog Spot who is not a man Spot who is a thing a thing a thing with no tongue I have your tongue Spot I have your tongue and I would eat it again if I could for I am the hunter of tongues and you are nothing Spot you aren't even Spot not really but I know who you are you cannot deceive me you motherfucker I know exactly who you are do you hear me?

"Do you hear me?" Mom's asking, somewhere far from here, somewhere impossible. "Mel, do you hear me?" But I can't respond. I have no tongue. I have no teeth. My lips are absent from my face and my face is absent from my skull and I am bones and I am ash and I am everything and I am nothing.

Bones creaking like twigs snapping in the night. Mom's above me and behind her are shadows and I can't understand why her skin is so bright, like it's glowing, like she's an insect caught in the galaxy, in the void of nothingness, and her bones are creak-creak-creaking, every time she moves her knees or elbows or neck, and she isn't alone, she's holding Bobby tight against her chest, chest against chest, and she's side-stepping around the bathroom, moving with such grace it's almost like they're floating, and they're dancing, dancing, dancing, but there's no music playing there's nothing the only sound is the creaking of bones, the creaking of bones, the creaking of bones, and Bobby's dead and decomposing and half a skeleton and his head keeps flopping every time our mother moves. Maggots fling out of his mouth and ears and eyes and vanish in the shadows. They're dancing just like they used to when he was alive, but now he's dead and nothing has changed, nothing ever changes. Somewhere in the darkness behind them, out of sight, Dad is screaming for me to let him use the flashlight on my phone, but it's too late, he's already lost it.

Together we're united in the circle of salt, wide enough to inhabit both our bodies, Amy and I, face to face, stripped of all clothing, maintaining eye contact like it's the last time we'll ever see each other. She slips a bronzed ring over her finger and it's so big it nearly slides back off. The insignia on the ring is beautiful and fascinating. Two winged creatures with exposed breasts levitating above a fountain, also looking each other in the eyes, much like Amy and I are doing, will never stop doing, staring like they love each other more than anything else the universe could possibly offer them, like they would do anything humanly possible and beyond to offer protection and prove their devout affection. I ask Amy about the ring and she tells me it's the seventh talisman from the *Black Pullet*. I ask where she got it from and she shakes her head, tells me some secrets aren't meant to be revealed and, before I can say anything else, she leans forward and kisses me for the last time and I tell her I love her. She retrieves a knife from outside the circle and punctures my flesh before I can protest. "Now me," she says. "Make me bleed." I press the blade against her arm and trace over an old scar. Blood drips down our flesh. We scoot closer so our limbs are locked around each other, forming a perfect Gordian knot in the center of the circle and, in my ear, Amy's whispering an incantation that makes me feel instantly at peace. Please god don't let this moment ever end. Please god please god please god.

VII. Has the power to destroy everything; to cause the fall of hail, thunderbolts, and stars of heaven; to occasion earthquakes, storms, and so forth. At the same time, it preserves the friends of the possessor from accidents. The figure of the talisman should be embroidered in silver upon poppy-red satin. The magic words are: (1) DITAU, HURANDOS, for works of destruction; (2) RIDAS, TALIMOL, to command the elements; (3) ATROSIS, NARPIDA, for the fall of hail, &c.; (4) UUSUR, ITAR, for earthquake; (5) HISPEN, TROMADOR, for hurricanes and storms; (6) PARANTHES, HISTANOS, for the preservation of friends.

Back in the bathroom, Amy's smiling at me from inside the cracked mirror. Her naked flesh pulsates like it's independent from her body. Throbbing. A bomb counting down to its inevitability. "I used to cut myself," her reflection says, mimicking the first sentence she ever spoke to me back in in-school suspension—and before I can respond, every scar on her body bursts in simultaneous celebration. Blood sprays through the mirror and splatters against my face. Small black tentacles peek out from the ruptured scars. Alien tree branches ascertaining whether the coast is clear before shedding its previous host and seeking shelter elsewhere. I try to scream and the tentacles bury themselves into my mouth before I'm able to make a sound.

Our phones won't stop screaming, each slightly out of sync with the other, making the noises jarring and insane.

We form a line and pile into the bathroom—Dad first, clutching an empty thermos; I'm behind him, every step forward painful, my legs itch so bad I can't stop it but I'm afraid to bend down and scratch them because what if my legs aren't there? what if legs are a lie and I believed it all this time?; behind me, Bobby staggers in, pupils missing from his eyes but that's okay, he's never had pupils anyway, and his breath reeks of something rancid, but he's always been bad about brushing his teeth, he's just a kid, kids suck at brushing their teeth, and in his hands he's holding Spot, Spot who hasn't stopped yelping since the storm began, Spot who's terrified of thunder, and he's so filthy, his fur's stained with wet mud and something red but I can't look at that, I can't; and last, behind Bobby and Spot, there's Mom, holding a pile of blankets against her chest as she shuts the door behind us, and inside the blanket something rattles, something almost like a snake, but what kind of mom would bring a rattlesnake into the bathroom with her family, what kind of sense would that even make? It's probably not a snake. It's probably just the wind.

"Oh my god," I shriek without opening my mouth, gripping my cell phone so tight I'm afraid it's going to break. The alert won't stop blaring. I turn it off and a new one takes its place. "*Why won't it stop?*" I finally open my mouth and blood pours down my chin like red paint from a tipped-over can.

Dad uncaps his thermos and hovers it under my jaw, letting the blood fill the container. "Just give it a second, would you?" Once it's full, he pops the lid back on and takes a long, pleasurable gulp through the mouth hole. He smiles and his teeth are red and he's never looked more content in his life.

Mom snaps her fingers until I look away from his teeth. The blanket's in the tub now, on top of Bobby, who's suddenly decided to take a nap. "Where were you? You should have been home by six."

"Mom, I don't feel good."

"Why weren't you answering my calls?"

"My stomach hurts, Mom. I think . . . I think something's wrong." I clutch my gut and double over, slowly lowering myself to the floor. An intense cramp burns inside me and it hurts to breathe. What is *happening* to me?

"You need to answer your phone when I call. That's why we pay for it every month."

"Mom, I think something's inside of me."

"Not good enough."

"We're all going to die because of you," Dad whispers, standing next to the closed bathroom door. His lips are red with my blood.

Mom turns to him. "What?"

"You didn't know your own daughter was a witch? Some fuckin' mother you are."

She looks back down at me. "Is this true, Mel?"

"Mom . . ." I raise my shirt up so they can see what I'm feeling. Something inside my stomach. Something moving back and forth. A small lump presses against my flesh. "Mom, help, please help."

"Don't," Dad says. "It's a trap. One of her witch traps. You try to help and she'll curse you."

"Something's *wrong!*" I scream, and grab the lump with both hands and squeeze and pull and my flesh begins ripping and blood erupts like a volcano from a fresh hole above my bellybutton and in my hands between my fingers the tongue I hunted and swallowed now writhes and attempts to flee, but I refuse to pardon it. "Where are you going?" I ask it, as blood continues gushing out of my stomach. "Where do you think you're going? You're mine. I caught you and now you're mine."

The tongue makes a noise like a tea kettle shrieking.

WE NEED TO DO SOMETHING

The tongue, I know this tongue like my own. It's Amy's tongue. I hunted it down and swallowed it up. She gave it to me and I refused to return it and now it's mine mine mine. If she really wants it back she'll have to personally come ask me.

Dad and Mom collapse to the floor and press their faces against my stomach, greedily slurping up the endless blood streaming out of me. They're so hungry, so thirsty, so desperate. I hold Amy's tongue above them and squeeze its juices into their hair. "This is my gift to you," I tell them. "This is my everything."

Behind us, in the bathtub, Bobby sits up and moans, "I think it's an EF5. I think it's an EF5. I think it's an EF5. I think it's—"

Somewhere outside, wind howls. Somewhere outside, thunder cracks. Somewhere outside, a tree falls, and it falls and it falls and it falls and it never, ever lands.

My stomach convulses violently as I vomit into the toilet. Behind me Mom holds my hair and rubs my back and promises everything is going to be okay. I swear to god a tongue splashes into the water and swims around like a fish that's finally returned home. When we flush it, the tongue screams with laughter and escapes the bathroom. Something we'll never be able to accomplish. Not now. Not ever. Unless the tongue sends help, but I don't think that's going to happen.

"Drink more water, honey. Please. You need to stay hydrated."

The three of us lay flat on our backs across the bathroom floor, staring at the ceiling, holding our stomachs. We look like shit. We smell like shit. We feel like shit. We are nothing but shit.

Then Dad says the unthinkable:

"We have to eat him."

Another long silence passes before Mom responds. "Go back to sleep."

"Either we eat him or we die."

"Then we die."

More nothingness.

Then Dad says, "I think I'm blind."

"What do you mean?" Mom asks.

"I can't fucking see anything anymore."

"What do you see?"

"Nothing. Fucking nothing."

"Oh." Mom sighs, half-awake. "It's probably those alcohol wipes. They can make you go blind if you ingest them."

"Why didn't you say anything?"

"Would you have cared?"

Dad struggles to sit up. Mom and I remain on our backs. He stands and approaches the tub, unwrapping the top of the blanket and grimacing as the scent intensifies. I start gagging but I'm too weak to do anything about it. He reaches down and feels around the body, although it's hard to decipher what exactly he's touching. Then he's gagging harder than I am and he backs away, hand over his mouth and nose.

Somehow Mom's already standing. "Leave him alone."

"It's our only choice," Dad says, eyes watery, voice cracking.

"Like hell it is."

"We have to."

He approaches the sink and touches the various items scattered along the sink counter, but it's obvious he can't see anything, not really. "Goddammit, where is it?"

"What are you doing?" Mom asks.

"We need something . . . something to cut open the flesh. The razor. What did you do with it?"

"Don't you fucking touch him."

Dad pauses and side-glances toward her, clearly annoyed. A thin stream of blood leaks out of his left eyeball. "Oh, would you stop acting so hysterical?"

He resumes his search awhile longer while Mom stares at him from across the bathroom, baffled. Finally, he gives up and takes off his shirt, at this point drenched with sweat and various other fluids. He wraps it around his fist and punches the mirror. Glass shatters into the sink basin and along the countertop. He cautiously feels around the glass, taking his time but also anxious, then wraps the T-shirt around the handle of a particularly long, thick shard.

He turns back toward the tub and Mom attempts to block his path but quickly retreats against the wall the moment he threatens her with his new weapon. Despite being blind, he can still sense her presence. He side-steps into the tub and crouches over the body, gripping the glass shard in one hand, holding it out, unsure how to proceed. He snarls at both of us like a cornered animal.

"If any of you . . . fucking *witches* . . . try to stop me . . . I won't . . . I don't know . . . we need to eat. Okay? We need to eat . . . we need to eat."

Dad cuts into Bobby's stomach and starts ripping out unrecognizable organs and eating them raw, taking huge animalistic bites and gagging as he chews. Mom and I remain on the opposite side of the bathroom, witnessing this atrocity and feeling totally helpless. I keep glancing at Bobby's face waiting for him to react.

But, of course, he doesn't react.

He can't.

And for that, I'm grateful.

Half a minute later, Dad's gagging gets out of control and he leaps from the tub, landing in the center of the bathroom on all fours and vomits everywhere. Blood and gore masks his face and finally we see his true form. He tries standing but slips in his own puke. More sickness projectiles out of his mouth as he screams. He gets up again and tackles the door, bounces off, lands in the puke again. Starts acting fully fucking crazy by standing, jumping at the door, falling, and doing it all over again for a long time, all the while spraying blood and vomit from his mouth. After several unsuccessful tackles, he crawls back to the door, pressing his face against the crack.

WE NEED TO DO SOMETHING

"Help! Heelllp! I'm being held prisoner by a coven of witches! A coven of witches has killed my boy! They've murdered my son in cold blood and I am next! Please! Pleeaase!"

He continues screaming nonsense for several minutes before going limp against the door and passing out. Mom and I don't dare move or make a sound. Neither of us are in much of a hurry to find out what happens next time he wakes up.

Noise explodes on the other side of the door. Dad jolts awake, snapping his head around the room, screaming. "I can't see anything! I can't fucking see! What's that fucking noise? What the fuck?"

"I don't know," Mom says. "Music, I think." She glances down at me, confused.

Of course I recognize the sound.

It's my phone.

Someone's calling me.

Amy.

You're alive.

Dad reaches through the door opening and feels around the carpet in their bedroom. "Oh, shit, I think I got it," he says, excited, and pulls my cell phone back into the bathroom with him.

Somehow it's survived through the rain.

Somehow the battery isn't dead.

I remain paralyzed across the room, unconvinced I'm not hallucinating again. This can't be real.

Can it?

Dad answers my phone and presses it against his ear, listening for a moment, and says, "Yes. Of course. Yes. No. I understand. Yes. Of course."

Then he snaps the phone and tosses the separated halves back through the door.

"What the fuck, Robert?" Mom says.

He starts slowly crawling across the bathroom, through vomit and blood and shit and piss, a lunatic smile carved across his face. "It makes sense, doesn't it?"

"Robert. Stop. Who did you talk to? Who called?"

He nods at me, somehow seeing me despite his recent loss of sight. "She's the one who caused this, which means she's the only one who can end it."

"Wh-what?" I whisper.

"Robert . . ."

He springs forward, wrapping his hands around my throat and slamming the back of my skull against the wall, screaming.

"*KILL THE WITCH KILL THE WITCH KILL THE WITCH!*"

Mom shouts somewhere nearby and tackles him off me. He rolls over on his back next to the toilet and Mom straddles his stomach, slapping his face with one hand after the other.

"*LEAVE HER ALONE LEAVE HER ALONE LEAVE HER ALONE!*"

The whole time she's hitting him, he's laughing loud and insane.

She leans to the side and knocks the toilet lid off the trash can, then flips over the container.

Only a second passes before the rattlesnake strikes out, somehow still alive, starving just like the rest of us, and latches its fangs onto Dad's left cheek.

He screams, this time in legitimate pain, and throws Mom off him like she weighs nothing.

He sits up. The snake remains hanging from his face. He won't stop screaming.

No, not screaming.

Laughing.

He's fucking laughing.

He rips the snake from his cheek and opens his mouth real wide and bites the creature's head clean off, then spits it toward Mom.

". . . kill the witch kill the witch kill the witch kill the witch . . ."

He stands, holding the decapitated snake's body, twirling it around like a lasso. Mom tries backpedaling while still on the floor but where the hell is she going to go?

". . . kill the witch kill the witch . . ."

He whips her with the snake, over and over, enjoying the sound of her screams.

Behind them, somehow, I manage to make it to my feet. In one hand I hold the glass shard he used to cut open Bobby's body, part of Dad's shirt still wrapped around the handle. The weapon's covered in blood and other things I can't dare to speculate on.

I raise it over my head and approach him, body trembling.

Once I begin stabbing him in the back, I don't stop until my arms are too heavy to lift, and by then he's long dead.

Mom and I retreat to the opposite side of the bathroom and sit against the wall. Mom's face is a shredded mess from the snake whippings. Looking at her makes me cry, so I stop looking at her.

We hold each other, shaking, and drift off into some definition of sleep.

I think Mom thinks I'm dead, and I don't know if she's wrong.

Eventually she abandons me against the wall and crawls over to Dad's mangled body. She scoops up the glass shard from his back, then crawls closer to the door and begins stabbing the wood. I don't know how long she does this. Hours. Days. Years. Time means nothing anymore. I can't move. I can't talk. Everything is so weak. If I'm not dead, then it'll happen soon enough. The glass slices into Mom's hands the longer she digs into the wood and blood leaks down and her face grimaces and she cries and screams and does not stop digging, and digging, and digging, and her cries are so loud and her blood is everywhere and still she digs, until finally the hole is just wide enough for a small, starving body to slip through.

"I'll come back, baby," she whispers. "I'll come back. Let me just . . . let me just see . . . "

She tosses the glass aside and doesn't waste a second before entering the new door.

A door within a door.

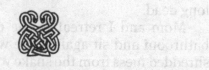

WE NEED TO DO SOMETHING

I wake up to something licking my hand. Spot is nestled in my lap, dirty and smelly but alive. I pet him and tell him he's a good boy and that I love him very much and fall back asleep. I do not ask how he got his tongue back. It would not be polite. When I wake up again, he's gone but my hand is still wet.

"Wake up," Amy's whispering. So close to my face I can feel her breath. It smells terrible. I open my eyes and she's in my lap. Nude and covered in dried blood. Her scars are no longer scars but split-open wounds.

Thin black tentacles keep her limbs attached to her body.

"Wake up, wake up, wake up."

I try telling her I'm awake but it's too hard to talk. She caresses my cheek. I desperately want her to kiss me.

Instead she nuzzles her face against my neck, relaxing in my limp embrace.

"You did all you could," she tells me. "Some people, they aren't meant to be fixed, no matter what you do. Some people are cursed from birth."

She squeezes my hand and I can feel her tears dripping down my chest.

I want to taste them so bad it hurts.

"None of this is your fault. It's nobody's fault. All you did was try to help."

She sits up again to look me dead in the eyes. The black tentacles slip in and out of her mouth, lifting her jaw up and down to form words.

"The truth is, Mel, you can't prevent the inevitable. No one can. All you can do is delay it for a little while."

Then she leans forward and I part my lips just wide enough to inhale her parasites and it's like we're kissing for the first time all over again.

Amy.

I love you so much.

Please don't leave me.

Loud breathing.

Crying.

Mom rushing back into the bathroom, eyes wide, a new energy to her face, tears down her cheeks.

Frantic.

She crawls through the bathroom, through the blood and vomit and shit smearing the floor, crawls back to me and grabs me tight and squeezes for dear life.

I don't know if I'm awake or asleep or alive or dead or what.

Amy's gone and I don't know if she was ever actually here.

I don't think it matters anymore.

Mom rocks us back and forth, refusing to look at the hole, at the door within a door, whispering,

"It's going to be okay it's going to be okay it's going to be okay it's going to be okay it's going to be okay it's going to be okay it's going to be okay it's going to be okay it's going to be okay it's going to be okay it's

going to be okay it's going to be okay it's going to be
okay it's going to be okay it's going to be okay it's
going to be okay it's going to be okay it's going to be
okay it's going to be okay it's going to be okay it's
going to be okay it's going to be okay it's going to be
okay it's going to be okay it's going to be okay it's
going to be okay it's going to be okay it's going to be
okay it's going to be okay it's going to be okay it's
going to be okay it's going to be okay it's going to be
okay it's going to be okay it's going to be okay it's
going to be okay it's going to be okay it's going to be
okay it's going to be okay it's going to be okay it's
going to be okay it's going to be okay it's going to be
okay it's going to be okay it's going to be okay it's
going to be okay it's going to be okay it's going to be
okay it's going to be okay it's going to be okay it's
going to be okay it's going to be okay it's going to be
okay it's going to be okay it's going to be okay it's
going to be okay it's going to be okay it's going to be
okay it's going to be okay it's going to be okay it's
going to be okay it's going to be okay it's going to be
okay it's going to be okay it's going to be okay it's
going to be okay it's going to be okay it's going to be
okay it's going to be okay it's going to be okay it's
going to be okay it's going to be okay it's going to be
okay it's going to be okay it's going to be okay it's
going to be okay it's going to be okay it's going to be
okay it's going to be okay it's going to be okay it's
going to be okay it's going to be okay it's going to be
okay it's going to be okay it's going to be okay it's
going to be okay it's going to be okay it's going to be

okay it's going to be okay it's

AUTHOR'S NOTE

What you just read was a book that saved my life. I self-released it through my small press, Perpetual Motion Machine Publishing, in April 2020 with almost zero pre-promotion or confidence that anybody would actually like it. At the time, I was nearing my eighth year working the night shift at a hotel on the city limits of San Antonio, which was a job I despised to my core (see my novel *The Nightly Disease* for a deeper exploration into this occupational hell). Just a reminder for those somehow reading this afterword years into the future: 2020 was not a particularly kind year for the human race. The coronavirus pandemic pretty much fucked us all.

For an idea of my mental state at the time, here is an email I sent my film & TV manager, Ryan Lewis, on March 20, 2020, at 4:53 AM:

Just wanted to let you know I'm leaning toward self-releasing this novella sometime soon. Something cheap and quick for people to read, an easy way to make some extra cash. Might be a good time for it, considering the novella is about a family caught in self-isolation from a natural disaster.

153

My hotel's cut some of my hours and let a bunch of other people go. I work for Marriott and I don't know if you've seen the news, but Marriott is facing a harder loss than they did for 9/11 and The Great Recession combined. It is looking pretty gloomy over here.

So that's why I'm leaning toward self-releasing it. I don't know how much longer I'll have a job and it will be an avenue to make a little bit of money.

How's it going with you and your family and everything?

My partner and I were barely managing to survive living paycheck-to-paycheck, which is the only lifestyle I've known since early into my childhood. Coworkers were getting furloughed left and right due to COVID complications. Our breakfast attendants and laundry person were let go, and both of their duties were suddenly sprung on me, without any additional payment. Several hotels near our location shut down. I was scared of losing my job while simultaneously terrified of catching COVID from handling dirty laundry or interacting with guests— where, in Texas, over half the population didn't believe the virus was even real. Not a shift went by that I didn't get into an argument with a guest refusing to wear a mask. My general manager at the hotel laughed and implied I was a coward whenever I brought up safety concerns. Misery plagued me every time I stood behind the front desk.

Before continuing, I should probably explain how

this novella originated in the first place. Contrary to how most books are written, *We Need to Do Something* started as a screenplay. Back in 2019, I had lunch with a screenwriter friend of mine named Shane McKenzie, who convinced me to try writing my own script so we could send it to an indie production company that was supposedly hungry for original material. Despite not having any experience with screenwriting, I decided to try it out with this weird bathroom idea I'd been thinking about.

Living in Central Texas means we often receive tornado warnings on our phones, although literally experiencing a tornado is pretty uncommon. At least by us. Still, it's better not to fuck with mother nature, right? So when the notifications do pop up, we seek shelter in our bathroom until the weather app tells us it's safe again. It was during one of these nights that I tried to spook my family by asking them a simple question: What would happen if we got stuck in here, and nobody came to help us? My partner's daughter immediately told me to shut up. All three of them acted unsettled by the question. I wasn't expecting them to actually take my joke seriously, but witnessing their reaction convinced me the premise could potentially respond well with an audience. At the very least, it would be a fun challenge to myself: Could I set an entire book within a bathroom? I'd previously written a novel primarily set inside a basement (*Carnivorous Lunar Activities*), so why not try a bathroom for the next one?

I already had this bathroom idea percolating before having lunch with my friend, but now it was all I could think about, because if we were going to send this script to an indie horror company, it was logical to assume they would prefer something that could be made with a low budget. I already knew this idea would be set in one room, with—at the very most—four characters. *They're going to love this!* I thought, while spending several months banging out a script. I sent it to my friend, who forwarded it to the film company. Then several more months passed without a response (to this day, they have not emailed us back about it).

When I first penned the screenplay, I did not have any representation. I wouldn't hook up with Ryan Lewis (my film & TV manager/guardian angel) until January 2020. But I knew how to (sorta) sell books, so I decided I would just stick with where I was more comfortable. I grew impatient and rewrote the script as a novella. This ended up being a great move on my part, because the novella vastly improved the original screenplay I wrote. For reference (I'm assuming you've at least read the book at this point), the original screenplay did not feature anything related to the supernatural. It also didn't contain any romance elements between Melissa and Amy. When I look back at it now, the screenplay served as a great outline for the eventual novella. Once I finished the book, I sent it out to a couple literary agents, but due to the word length (36,000) nobody would even look at it. Agents don't really care about novellas. They want novels with a minimum length of 60,000 words. This book didn't stand a chance. So I sat on it for a couple months, unsure what to do with it.

Then, well, 2020 happened. Go reread the email I sent Ryan Lewis if you need a refresher.

I didn't think self-releasing *We Need to Do*

AFTERWORD

Something would help my situation *that* much, to be fair. There is not a lot of money in indie horror. I figured, at the most, it'd refuel our cars or restock our house with groceries a couple times. As it turned out, however, I was never fired from the hotel. Deeper into the summer, our murderous governor, Greg Abbott, lifted the minimal COVID restrictions already in place, and the hotel tried resuming as if business was perfectly normal and people weren't wheezing their final breaths around the globe from a virus without—at the time— any vaccine available. The stress had finally reached a boiling point and, after discussing the situation with my partner, Lori Michelle, we decided I would put my two weeks' notice in and try to make a living with writing, publishing, and various freelance gigs.

I should also note that this decision was made in August 2020, one month after optioning *We Need to Do Something* to Atlas Industries for $5,000 (read Sean King O'Grady's wonderful introduction for further details on how that came about), but we had no way of knowing whether or not it would actually get funded. Books get optioned all the time and nothing ever happens with them. I didn't think for a second that I would somehow be the exception. The money we were seeking for the budget ($800,000), while small compared to most other movies, seemed like an impossible number in my eyes. The script that we sold to Atlas Industries was a new version of the story, separate from the original screenplay I tried writing back in 2019, now incorporating elements created for the novella version. I wrote this new script in the early months of 2020, with Ryan providing many necessary notes on how to improve it.

However, with that said, exactly one week after turning in my notice at the hotel, we received a phone call from Ryan, informing us the movie had miraculously received full funding, and we would begin shooting in late September. Meaning I would get paid the remaining purchase price on day one of filming: $35,000, more money than I had ever seen in my life. Meaning I wouldn't need to let freelance stress give me a heart attack at the age of 27. Lori and I celebrated by eating Whataburger, which—ironically—was probably more likely to cause a heart attack than anything else. Actually, come to think about it, I think we were on the way home from picking up Whataburger when Ryan called us, so maybe the terrible-yet-delicious food decision had nothing to do with our good news. Holy shit now I'm craving Whataburger again.

Anyway, a lot happened between initially optioning the book and physically filming the adaptation, but if I tried covering every detail, this afterword would quickly exceed the length of the novella. I was fortunate to work with people who valued my opinion, and let me contribute on decisions beyond writing, such as set production and casting ideas (I was the one who introduced everybody to Sierra McCormick, after watching *The Vast of Night*; she would go on to play Melissa in *WNTDS*). Let's just say I probably have another book's worth of email exchanges between myself, Ryan Lewis, Sean King O'Grady, Bill Stertz, Amy Williams, and Josh Malerman, as we all figured out exactly how we would make this thing.

So, in the beginning of October, now a full-time

AFTERWORD

writer, I drove from San Antonio, Texas, to Southfield, Michigan, and quarantined in a hotel for a month with the cast and crew as we all made a movie together. I juggled my time between hanging out on set and sitting with our editor, Shane Patrick Ford, as he pieced together the movie while everybody else filmed the day's scenes directly below in our garage-turned-soundstage. Every night I returned to my hotel room exhausted and beyond excited to do it all over again the next day. Except for the night I drank an entire bottle of Knob Creek while partying with some of the crew. I may have spent the following day vomiting in my hotel room and praying for a quick death. Luckily, I had already stocked up on plenty of saltine crackers, otherwise I might not be alive today to write this afterword.

It was an insane time. Probably the best month of my life. I think about it constantly and hope to experience it again and again and again. I am writing this exactly one month before IFC Midnight releases the film in theaters and video-on-demand. I don't know if people are going to like it. I don't know if it's going to make or break my career in screenwriting. Much like the family in *We Need to Do Something*, I don't know much of anything right now, except for the fact that in July 2020 I virtually met Sean King O'Grady, who told me he wanted to direct my screenplay, and almost one year later the film was complete and debuting at Tribeca Film Fest in Brooklyn, and now next month it's releasing to the public—in goddamn *theaters*. People dream about this stuff and never come close to experiencing it and here it is, actually happening. The only real lesson I've learned from any of this is that life is nuts and unpredictable and nothing makes sense.

If you read this book and/or watched the movie, I hope—at the very least—it made you feel something. If it bored you, then I've failed. I can't confidently say it's a great work of literature, or a cinematic masterpiece, but I can promise you one thing: it's not boring. So thank you for your time. I hope it wasn't wasted.

Max Booth III
August 03, 2021

ABOUT THE AUTHOR

Max Booth III is the Editor-in-Chief of Perpetual Motion Machine and the Managing Editor of *Dark Moon Digest*. Listen to his podcast, Ghoulish, by pressing your ear against the nearest bleeding wound. Connnect with him on Twitter @GiveMeYourTeeth or his website at www.TalesFromTheBooth.com. Please wash your hands after reading this book.

IF YOU ENJOYED
WE NEED TO DO SOMETHING,
DON'T MISS THESE OTHER TITLES FROM
PERPETUAL MOTION MACHINE . . .

THE NIGHTLY DISEASE
BY MAX BOOTH III
ISBN: 978-1-943720-24-8
$18.95

Sleep is just a myth created by mattress salesmen. Isaac, a night auditor of a hotel somewhere in the surreal void of Texas, is sick and tired of his guests. When he clocks in at night, he's hoping for a nice, quiet eight hours of Netflix-bingeing and occasional masturbation. What he doesn't want to do is fetch anybody extra towels or dive face-first into somebody's clogged toilet. And he sure as hell doesn't want to get involved in some trippy owl conspiracy or dispose of any dead bodies. But hey . . . that's life in the hotel business. Welcome to The Nightly Disease. Please enjoy your stay.

LIKE JAGGED TEETH
BY BETTY ROCKSTEADY
ISBN: 978-1-943720-21-7
$12.95

The guys following her home are bad enough, but when Jacalyn's Poppa comes to the rescue, things only get worse. After all, he's been dead for six years. There's no time to be relieved, because when she ends up back at Poppa's new apartment, nothing feels right. The food here doesn't taste how food should taste. The doors don't work how doors are supposed to work. And something's not right with Poppa. Guilt and sickness spiral Jacalyn into a nightmarish new reality of Lynchian hallucinations and grotesque body horror.

TOUCH THE NIGHT
BY MAX BOOTH III
ISBN: 978-1-943720-47-7
$18.95

Something sinister's hiding in the small town of Percy, Indiana, and twelve-year-old Joshua Washington and Alonzo Jones are about to find themselves up close and personal with it. After a harmless night of petty property damage leads to the unthinkable, the red and blue lights of a cop car are the last things these boys want to see. Especially a cop car driven by something not quite human.

Enter Mary Washington and Ottessa Jones. Their sons have been best friends for years, and now Josh and Alonzo have been abducted in the dead of night. Worst of all, the local sheriff refuses to believe they're missing, leaving it up to Mary and Ottessa to take the law into their own hands before a family of ungodly lunatics can complete a ritual decades in the making.

Together they will embark on a surreal and violent journey into a land of corrupt law enforcement, small-town secrets, gravitational oddities, and ancient black magic.

The Perpetual Motion Machine Catalog

Antioch | Jessica Leonard | Novel

Baby Powder and Other Terrifying Substances | John C. Foster | Story Collection

Bone Saw | Patrick Lacey | Novel

Born in Blood Vols. 1 & 2 | George Daniel Lea | Story Collections

Crabtown, USA:Essays & Observations | Rafael Alvarez | Essays

Dead Men | John Foster | Novel

The Detained | Kristopher Triana | Novella

Eight Eyes that See You Die | W.P. Johnson | Story Collection

The Flying None | Cody Goodfellow | Novella

The Girl in the Video | Michael David Wilson | Novella

Gods on the Lam | Christopher David Rosales | Novel

The Green Kangaroos | Jessica McHugh | Novel

Invasion of the Weirdos | Andrew Hilbert | Novel

Jurassichrist | Michael Allen Rose | Novella

Last Dance in Phoenix | Kurt Reichenbaugh | Novel

Like Jagged Teeth | Betty Rocksteady | Novella

Live On No Evil | Jeremiah Israel | Novel

Lost Films | Various Authors | Anthology

Lost Signals | Various Authors | Anthology

Mojo Rising | Bob Pastorella | Novella

Night Roads | John Foster | Novel

The Nightly Disease | Max Booth III | Novel

Quizzleboon | John Oliver Hodges | Novel

The Ruin Season | Kristopher Triana | Novel

Scanlines | Todd Keisling | Novella

Patreon:
www.patreon.com/pmmpublishing

Website:
www.PerpetualPublishing.com

Facebook:
www.facebook.com/PerpetualPublishing

Twitter:
@PMMPublishing

Newsletter:
www.PMMPNews.com

Email Us:
Contact@PerpetualPublishing.com